My Escape to Loon Haven

By Sylvia Duncan

Best wishes!
Sylvia Duncan

ISBN: 9798354653560

Chapter 1

The gray, metal door swings open suddenly with a bang sounding like a gunshot. I squat as low as I can, jeans straining at the knees, and yank my black hoodie over my face. I have to hide. If the manager catches me, I could be arrested for stealing food from his gross, smelly dumpster. He threatened, swore, and pushed me against the enclosure wall the last time he caught me taking a kid's meal from a box that was barely touched by some child who just wanted the toy, not the chicken nuggets, milk and apple slices I desperately needed. Now, I hear footsteps and the sour smell of cigarette smoke. Probably not the manager, who doesn't need to come to the back of the parking lot to dump trash and to smoke, but I can't take any chances on an underpaid rat on a power trip grabbing me and turning me in. I have no choice now but to stay here, silent, shivering, tennis shoes mired in a rancid, greasy puddle, and hope against hope he or she will leave before my tired legs give me away. *Go away, go away…please, go away.*

My heart is pounding, and I am desperate to make a dash for it, but my heart and legs just won't cooperate. I'm too discouraged, tired, and hungry to run. I close my eyes and my foggy brain summons up advice from my uncle, who used to teach me how to sit quietly and to wait for the wild animals to emerge in the evening at his cabin. *Pay attention to your breathing, Jenna. That's all that matters. Calmly in through your nose, out through your mouth. Count to ten over and over. One…two…three.*

Before long, my shoulders relax and I don't feel so much like throwing up.

One…two…three…four. I hear muffled rap music from the earbuds of the person leaning against the other side of the dumpster. Still there, for gosh sakes! I have to push away the fear and accept my situation here, I guess.

Everything is so stupid. Acceptance, fear, and stress all the time—that's the story of my life. I'm not where I want to be. I have no choices. I have no friends. I'm wearing church hand-me-downs. I hate school, not because I don't like to learn, but not much learning goes on in that ugly brick building. The constant lies and deceptions make my stomach knot up. Nagging, always nagging and pushing. Coach: Jenna, you are a natural athlete. You should try out for basketball. Me: Oh, no, I am needed at home after school. English Teacher: I would love to see more of your writing. Email it to me sometime. Me: I would like to, but my computer is broken. All the ridiculous school chatter, and I lie and lie, 24/7, it seems.

What they all don't know is that this scared, uberskinny white girl folds her long legs into the back seat of a dingy Buick every night, pulls a worn, pink comforter up over her ears, and tries to muffle the sounds of her mother reclining in the front seat and whimpering in pain until she finally passes out. Mom runs the heater once in a while when it is super cold out. This has been our life for three months since our landlord kicked us out on the street. Visits to soup kitchens and dumpster diving have been the only way to stay alive in these past miserable months—late winter into spring, wet, windy and super crappy every day and night. Mom's addiction to painkillers is bad, but she can't afford to stay drugged up all of the time, so the in between times are really dangerous for her.

Shelters don't work for us with her addiction, and she stubbornly refuses to get treatment because we are both afraid they will put me in foster care. Adding to that is a heart condition the free clinic has told her about. She is drowning in pain and numbed reality, and I have been getting slowly sucked down with her year by year, month by month, day by day.

The thing that worries me the most: I take care of my mother but I don't feel the love anymore. In fact, I don't know if I know what love really is. She is fading away from me, and I am left to take care of both of us all by myself. I don't know how to do it. I don't WANT to do it!

The only safety we feel is Dave, our former neighbor, takes pity on us and lets us park our car at night in his locked impound lot that has a restroom with a toilet and sink. During the day, I carefully move our car to the street. I volunteer to shovel gray, sloppy slush and keep his office sidewalk clear and the bathroom clean in the hope he will continue to let us park there overnight until some fricking miracle comes along. He doesn't ask for anything more from me or my mom…and, for that, I am grateful. At least I don't have to lie to him and can look him in the eye without fear. He is the only person who knows the truth of our lives, and he has never laid a hand on Mom or me. He has a wife and daughters of his own.

"Jenna, is that you?" A dark and shadowy face peeks around the dumpster, jerking me back from my deep thoughts. I draw back and hit my head on the cold metal with a thump.

The voice goes on, "It's Jordan, Jenna. I thought I recognized those pink tennis shoes of yours stickin' down there when I threw in the trash. Don't tell my moms I bum a cigarette once in a while. Come on out and I'll share my dinner." He sees me hesitate and softly urges me, as if I'm a scared puppy. "It's okay. I would never rat on you. I get free food on my breaks. Guess that is one good thing about putting in my time slinging burgers, and, they are so hard up, they made ME a crew leader." He chuckles to try to put me at ease. My complaining stomach draws me up and forward toward the aroma of hot fries in the grease-stained brown bag. He extends it toward me with a smile.

"Didn't see you in the halls today. Everything okay? I know the ballers' girlfriends were giving you a hard time the other day. Don't pay any attention to them—especially Sheila. She gets her kicks intimidating all the freshman girls, but you are a prime target because—well, I guess I don't need to spell it out. Join the Robotics Club with all the geeks like me. No one would hassle you there, for sure. One of the big corporations just sent us a box of awesome stuff to write code and program. You're smart and would dig it.

"Whatcha doing hiding back here anyways? Is someone after you?"

I take the bag from him and it warms my chilly fingers, "I'm trying to get food for my mom. She's sick."

"What?"

"Yeah. It sucks. She needs me."

I watch him think about this for a moment. "Do you live around here?"

"In a white Buick parked down a couple of blocks." I peek into the bag and my mouth begins to water.

"Oh, man." He shakes his head slowly and sighs. "Didn't know that. Too bad, kid. Hey, eat up. I always get enough for two people on my dinner—getting fat and greasy at this job. Next thing you know, everyone will be calling me Lard Ass."

I dig into the fries like a junkyard dog. No pride. The saltiness satisfies a desperate craving. I will save a burger for Mom, if she can eat it. If not, it will be breakfast for me tomorrow.

Jordan watches me as I snarf down his dinner. He has a thoughtful, pained look on his face. "Jenna, tell you what. How 'bout I meet you here at seven every evening for a while until you get back on your feet? I thought me and my moms was just scraping by, but at least we have an apartment. What else can I do?"

My eyes narrow in suspicion, and I mumble around a big mouthful of hamburger, "Why do you ask that?"

"What do ya mean?"

"Usually when the men around my mother offer to help there's a catch, a BIG catch, if you get what I'm sayin'."

He steps back as if I have slapped him. "Oh, man, I don't mean that, Jenna. Getting paid back THAT way is the last thing on my mind. I've just always kinda liked you…wondered why you weren't out in the 'burbs…think you are brave to keep coming to my school. Our school sucks, but decent SAT and ACT scores are my tickets out of here, so I keep going."

"Well, okay, but we understand each other, right?"

He gives me a big, toothy grin, "Yes, ma'am!"

He tosses in another bag of trash and hustles back to work, leaving his dinner with me. He hasn't eaten a thing.

My heart slows. The edge has gone off my hunger and fear talking to Jordan. I guess he's okay for a boy.

Chapter 2

At night my mind whirls, the street lights glare in my eyes, sirens shriek, and the occasional gunshot rings out on the street. I haven't slept more than a few hours at a time for months. I think I'm going to explode with worry and stress. I want to be a little kid again so bad. I want to have a warm bed and good food in a big white refrigerator. I want to ride my pink bike on the wide sidewalk in front of our little ranch house with the neighbor kids, climb trees, play kickball, and ride a big yellow bus to a warm, safe school. I want a pink backpack and a cubby with my name on it to hang it in, and my blonde hair in braids. I want to stand in front of my mom as her warm, loving hands comb and part and tug my head this way and that, as she softly hums a tune…..

Leaves have finally popped out on the trees. Mom seems to be feeling a little better, but her face is so gray. She's still bundling up in her winter coat, hat, and gloves to keep from shivering. I'm trying my darndest to finish up the school year. I legally have to be in school. I actually want to learn about science, to check books out of the library, and to shower and shampoo twice a week after gym class. Other than that, I don't care to sit tall and white in a classroom where I literally stick out like a sore thumb. I get a lot of stares at my blonde hair and pale complexion. I feel like an animal in the zoo, as if these kids haven't ever seen a real live white person. Maybe they haven't, except on TV and in a police uniform. I get plenty of harassment about it, especially from the mean girls who seem afraid I'm going to steal their boyfriends. As if. I need a boyfriend like a hole in the head, but it makes me sad and angry to keep my eyes down, fists clenched, boiling inside and trying to stay off the radar of the bullies. I can't afford to get into trouble even if I am itching to give some payback when I'm elbowed into the hallway lockers.

Guess I do have one friend. The combination of the free breakfast and lunch at school and Jordan's sack dinners most evenings has helped me feel stronger, and the spring sunshine gives me hope that maybe Mom and I can survive another season. I don't know how, but we can't spend another brutal winter living like animals.

Chapter 3

Thank God the public library is open. I rush up the wide steps and hurry by the front desk, head down so she can't see my tears. The librarian is distracted with customers, and I slip by unnoticed. The cracked leather chair in my private corner behind the far bookshelves is waiting for me. I kick off my shoes and curl up in its familiar, warm embrace…safe here. Outside the high window, the tops of tall trees sway in the wind.

Get ahold of yourself, Jenna. Breathe. My hands hurt so bad. I have clenched my fists so hard for so long there are four bloody arches in my palms from my fingernails digging into my flesh. The cuts look nasty, but not serious. I feel pins and needles as I flex my fingers. That sore spot behind my ear…oww oww! My finger comes back covered with crusted blood. OMG! Hot tears splash down onto my coat. My heart and stomach ache right now, and I cannot think straight.

If I hug my knees and close my eyes tight enough maybe I will get my wish and just disappear. I want to forget Sheila's eyes, full of hatred as she grabbed my hair and spun me around in the crowded hallway. Her loud snarl as she announced to everyone, "Hey, white girl, show me that red neck of yours. Why you talk like one of them hillbillies when you open your mouf? You born in some barn?"

"Fight! Girl fight!" When I shoved her away, a bunch of my long hair was caught in one of her big rings and was ripped from my head. A teacher pushed his way through the crowd and held us apart. Sheila kept taking wild swings at me. The air was electric with hatred. My heart thumped in my ears. The bell mercifully rang and kids slowly grumbled off to class…disappointed they didn't get to see me on the floor. The hall was empty except for the two of us and the middle-aged man.

"This white hillbilly don't belong in our school, you know that Mr. Wilson. She don't do nothing in class, just sits and stares at me and my friends, she acting all high and mighty."

Fat Mr. Wilson, his ebony skin glistening from exertion, listened without speaking, but his weary eyes and wrinkled brow told me, down deep, he agreed with her. They both turned. He walked Sheila to the door of her class, leaving me standing alone, holding back tears of rage and pain. That was it. Over. Just like that. So unfair.

When my head cleared, I realized she, or someone like her, would be back for me. I grabbed my coat from my shabby locker, slammed it shut, and left school right then. No waiting around for anyone to follow me after school and push me into doing something I would regret forever. I can't afford to get in trouble. No one can or will protect me. My feet automatically brought me here, to my safe thinking spot in the warm and quiet public library.

The water is finally running clear in the restroom sink. I'm a little dizzy as I lean over to dry my hair at the hand dryer. A cereal bar from the free school breakfast is in my coat. Revived by oats, chocolate, and a long drink from my cupped hands, I leave the restroom, grab a random book off the shelf, and sink back into my chair, using my coat as a blanket. People are welcome to stay in the library as long as they wish, if they are quiet, have a book open in front of them and are not asleep, although I don't think the kind librarian has ever thrown out a sleeper. I have often listened as she goes around at closing, gently and quietly asking each person where he or she is going to get dinner and a bed on a cold winter night. She will make a call once in a while and a van from social services will stop by the curb to deliver people to shelter for the night, sometimes in church basements. The next morning, after a free breakfast and a hot shower, they walk back to the library where there is warmth, safety, and friends who look out after each other. When she asks me, of course, I lie.

My brain is finally kicking in. Mom and I can't do this anymore. Sheila has pushed me over the edge. I can't go back to school. It's dangerous and lame. We've got to get out of the city. Mom isn't in any kind of shape to make decisions, so I've got to figure this out myself, and I've got to do it now. I'm fourteen going on fifty, and I hate my life more today than ever.

I pull my coat up to my chin, sink into the soft leather and try to remember the last time I wasn't under stress…when others were protecting and taking care of me instead of the other way around. The memories are dark and far away, but, if I slow my heartbeat and sit perfectly still, the voices of three people come to me and comfort me. I have no photos from my early years, but my memories are their voices.

"*We don't fight or swear in this house. Count to ten, dear.*" Grandma.

"*Come on, Jenna. Don't set that bucket down, dang it. You are tough. You can do hard things.*" Grandpa.

"*Trust yourself.*" Uncle Bill.

Grandma's house was quiet. Warm in the winter and cool in the summer. I played in the garden as Grandma planted, watered, weeded, and picked the veggies. She hummed as she worked. Church tunes, I guess. Mom and Dad had jobs working in the local trailer factory. Mom sewed curtains and other things and Dad worked on the line with a big tool that joined the wood together. They never told me much about their jobs. When they got home they were tired. I overheard enough to know they argued about everything. I got scared sometimes. Mom was mad she was "stuck" on the farm. Dad argued back that his folks needed their help because the bank owned the farm.

Meanwhile, I grew up a quiet, little kid, listening to all the conversation around the edges….soaking in the tone of conversations, the country way of saying things and putting them to memory. I could sit in a room with a book and everyone talked as if I were invisible. Sheila wanted to know if I was born in a barn. She wasn't far off with what she thought was an insult but what were really the authentic voices of good people…people of the land, of church, of Indiana grandparents and Uncle Bill's northern Michigan. Their combined voice is mine…and it is all I know. I'm a good person. They tell me so. I can't scream obscenities down a hallway and think I am funny. Grandma won't let me. I can't give up and be nasty to everyone. Grandpa won't let me. I can't be less than my best. Uncle Bill won't stand for it. If that's weird, well, call me weird.

After they died…Grandma from illness and Grandpa from a broken heart...Mom explained good jobs were waiting for her and Dad in Gary. She would have her dream of being close to Chicago, and we could live in a place with other children to play with. I would get a bike, and she would take me to the Science and Industry Museum as soon as we got settled.

She was good for her word. I had little girlfriends, a room of my own, a good school, a bike, and summers with Uncle Bill up north. Blonde braids, smiles in the mirror, hugs. Tears come again, and I wipe my eyes with my sleeve. There it was. That was it. From six to ten I was warm and safe. The last happy time of my life before it all fell apart. Just four stinking years to be a carefree little girl.

Dad died in a horrible car crash on the interstate. Mom injured herself on the job and started with pain meds. It wasn't fair to stop having sleepovers and trips to museums. I came home from school to an empty house and let myself in with a hidden key. Mom started coming home later and later, and she was always either on the edge of tears, unwilling to talk, or angry at me for just being in her way. I tried to make something for both of us to eat from the few things in the fridge or pantry, but she was generally out of it. I thought she was just tired, but now I know the drugs were taking over her life. She would leave the sandwich I made for her and go straight to bed. I learned to get along without her, and many days could go by when we didn't even see each other. My summers in Michigan ended with no explanation when I was eight, though I cried and begged to go…to get away from her…to feel loved again. She refused to call Uncle Bill.

One crappy apartment without even a cell phone and one dingy Buick later and here I am: scared, drained, hurting inside and out, and feeling like I've finally hit rock bottom.

"*Say a prayer.*" Grandma. I never got the hang of it. Sorry.

"*Straighten that mother of yours out.*" Grandpa. If you only knew how I have tried.

"*Stay calm. Breathe. Think and see clearly.*" Uncle Bill. Oh, how I wish you were here, Uncle Bill! I need you so much.

I don't have a fricking clue what I will do when I walk out that door onto the city streets.

Chapter 4

A cop car speeds by me. The siren is screaming, sound bouncing off all the tall buildings. Another car, light bar flashing, comes to a screeching stop. Nothing to be surprised about in the early evening on the Chicago streets, but the feelings of bad things happening to anyone always sets off something in my brain and ties a double knot in my stomach. Strobe lights flash, red emergency vehicles rush in, uniformed cops and guys in white hazmat suits are milling around in front of the alley near our car. Outraged drivers, trying to get home from work, lay on their horns. I finger the car keys in my pocket—a nervous habit I have acquired as I have, time after time, considered the possibility we would have to move our car and Mom would not be able to tell me where she put her keys. The chunk of cold metal and plastic is my lifeline, and my adrenaline kicks into high gear. *Stay calm, Jenna. Think!*

I step into a doorway where I can see but not be seen. The sirens have stopped, and the silence is deafening. I watch men and women moving in what seems to be slow motion through the flashing lights. A cop is radioing and I overhear his scratchy conversation.

"What's the situation down there?"

"Oh, some druggie was found dead in the alley by a passerby. Doc thinks it was a heart attack that did her in, though. He can tell us more later. We're about to move the body and get the street opened up again."

"Yeah, let's get that traffic movin'. Drivers are gripin' to the switchboard already. You say a woman?"

"Yeah."

"Identification?"

"No clue."

I have to think fast. I have rehearsed this possibility in my brain a hundred times as I lay listening to Mom's labored breath and fitful groans. I have to pull this off and I don't have much time. I take three deep breaths, run a hand through my hair, stand up straight and step confidently toward the cop. I've had a lot of experience lying in the last few years, but this is the most important lie of my life.

"Officer, I can see you have some sort of situation here, but I need to get something for my dad out of our family car over there." I point in the general direction of the Buick. "He is a lawyer and has a meeting with an apartment owner. He sent me down to get some important papers for him."

He looks me over and scowls at me. "Well, you had better make it snappy and keep out of the way, kid."

"Ok. It will only take a sec."

It is a sinking feeling to know what I will see when I get close to the alley. Mom isn't in the car. I catch a glimpse of a familiar flannel jacket as they are readying to carry her body to the ambulance. I am frozen at the sight. I can't run to her. I don't want to run to her. I know what I immediately have to do before they search the license number and figure out from all the junk in our car that it belongs to her. It will be towed and impounded. I am a horrible daughter, but I have rehearsed this situation on many sleepless nights, when I wondered what if…

Willing myself to look as mature and calm as possible, I manage to unlock the car door with shaking hands, to get the key in the ignition, to start the engine, and to cruise slowly away from the curb. I'm not a total stranger to driving this big car. Several times, in desperation, Mom had convinced me to drive around and around the busy downtown blocks after dropping her off to buy painkillers. She would meet me at the curb after her score and slip into the driver's seat. *Please, God, don't let that cop be watching me.* I glance at his shrinking figure in my rear view mirror. *Oh, man, what do I do now?*

Steering carefully in the right hand lane, I drive three city blocks on green lights, make a right hand turn into the first familiar place I spot, and squeeze the car into a tight parking space. My heart is pounding and every nerve in my body is on high alert. I close my eyes and feel the hot tracks of tears coursing down my cheeks. Sadness for my mom and her screwed up life. The prescription drugs that killed her. Sadness for our lost life and the waste of it all.

I pull my pink comforter from under all the stuff in the back seat, recline to make myself invisible, and let the tears fall—sobbing now—no way to hold back. My head feels like it is about to explode. My heart is being clamped tighter and tighter, and I feel a deep ache in every muscle. Heartbreak hurts, weighs a ton, and presses me deeper and deeper down.

Chapter 5

I startle awake at the sound of my own strangled cry. For a moment, I have no idea where I am, pinned behind the steering wheel by something or someone suffocating me. Reality streams back to me as I frantically tear away the tangled comforter from my chest and throat. As I begin to remember where I am and why I am here, my heartbeat slows and I realize my coma-like sleep has actually done me good, and I am thinking more clearly: not as cold, not as shocky. I have awakened in survival mode now—my survival—no one else's. I have a foggy notion of a crazy plan, but I need help. First things first. When we were tossed out of our apartment, I found four fifty dollar bills Mom had hidden in a kitchen cupboard. I secretly tucked them in a small tear in the upholstery of the passenger seat as super emergency money, not to go for drugs. I lift the arm rest and feel around. The crinkle of bills. Yes! They are still there. Some weight lifted from my aching heart, and I sink back in relief.

It must be super late, as the small night crew is just mostly chilling out in Jordan's brightly lit fast food joint. Employees are looking for things to do to make the shift go faster, doing a half-assed job swabbing down the linoleum floors and wiping tables. I'm lucky I steered to this familiar place. I stuff the faded comforter into the passenger seat and watch as an older woman fills the napkins and checks the condiments.

I turn in the seat and hug my knees to my chest, head against the side window. Shivering, my heart sinks as I realize I am totally alone in this world. Two hundred dollars to my name and a rusty junker full of all I own. The sum total of my life: past, present, and future. Back seat for clothes with room carved out for sleeping. Foot well crammed with shoes and boots. Trunk a jumble of the tent, a box of canned goods from the local food pantry, toilet paper, soap, shampoo, and towels. Pillows, Mom's sleeping bag, a plastic bag of costume jewelry in the glove box along with aspirin and our toothbrushes. I struggle to sit up straight behind the wheel again. I gotta get out of here before some cop puts two and two together and I end up some poor orphan kid in foster care: a live-in teenage babysitter for a bunch of snotty toddlers at risk from a man I don't know. I've overheard too many stories from the other kids.

I pull the plastic bag from the glove box and run my hand through Mom's jewelry. I remember her wearing these jade earrings and the matching ring. She came to a science fair and looked so pretty. I was proud she was my mom in that happy stretch of our lives. Now, I am feeling a weird, numb disconnect from her. My weeping has left me emptied out, and I can't even get a clear picture of her face. Is it totally crazy to mainly be feeling a sense of relief? That's wrong—totally wrong, isn't it? Isn't it? But the heartache is lessening and this strange sense of emptiness and numbness is taking its place. I remind myself over and over—I have to trust myself now—no one else.

Wait! Jordan is working the night shift! He's in there putting up new posters on the front windows—pictures of giant pancakes swimming in syrup, unnaturally bright yellow scrambled eggs, and huge, steaming coffees to draw in the hungry and thirsty. I'm so lucky he is working tonight. I wave and he leans forward over a table and peers out the window into the shadowy parking lot. He's smiling. He recognizes me! I gesture to him to come out and mouth the words. I don't want to get out of the car because I have no idea if there are still cops around who would wonder why I am not in the suburbs somewhere drinking hot cocoa while finishing my homework—in my pajamas—in a warm room with the household cat curled up on my bed. What a fantasy. Wish it were true, though, and I wasn't such a miserable wreck.

He approaches the car and I roll down the window. "Listen, Jordan, I need your help."

"God, you look horrible, Jenna. What's up?"

"My mom just died on the street and I have to get out of here."

"What? She died? What do you mean get out of here? Where the heck do you think you're going to go? You don't even have your driver's license. It's the middle of the night! You need to let the cops know you are by yourself."

I pull back and start to roll up the window. I should have known he isn't going to help me. He grasps the top of the window glass and pleads, "Hold on! Don't get mad. Wait until my shift is over. We'll go to my place and ask my moms what you should do. She's cool about stuff and wouldn't hit the panic button. You could hang out there fo.........."

"No, thanks, Jordan." I interrupt him. "Getting hung up in the system is not in the plans. That's nice and all, but what I really want to know is if you have any extra money you could spare me. I wouldn't ask, but you are the only person I know and trust."

He looks seriously at me. I return his gaze. I won't blame him one bit if he turns around and leaves me sitting here, but it's a long shot I have to take. He is silent for a while, but then he takes a deep breath. He has made a painful decision. He hardly knows me. I reach for the dangling car keys. I might as well get out of here.

"Hold on, Jenna. I just cashed my paycheck after school today. I owe my moms for my part of our phone bill. I mean, I hardly really know you, and I'm probably nuts to do this, but I'm going to give you the $60 I have in my pocket. It's the best I can do, Jenna. I really, really think you're doing the totally wrong thing here. I'm not feelin' this, Jenna. I'm scared for you."

I reply quietly, breathing normally for the first time in hours, "I'm totally desperate or you know I would never ask, Jordan. With the little money I have on hand and your $60, I should be able to get a new start." I turn to the jewelry box on the seat. "I want to give you something. You have been a good friend the last couple of months. Here is a set of earrings and a ring that would look great on your mom. They aren't worth $60, but I'll send your money to you as soon as I get settled somewhere and find a job. Promise. You can give the jewelry to your mom right now for keeps. I'd rather not see it ever again, honestly."

Jordan turns the jewelry over and over in his hand for a long time, and then reaches deep into his front pocket and comes out with three neatly folded $20 bills. He hands them over with obvious reluctance. He worked hard at a crummy job for that money, but I will pay him back sooner than later. I know I will.

"You sure you won't hang out for a while at my house, Jenna?"

"No, thanks. I'm gonna leave right now."

"Any idea where you are going?"

"I've got an idea, but I'd rather not say."

"Well. Call me sometime, will ya?"

I lean out the window, hug his neck, and give him a peck on his warm, stubbly cheek. "You're the best, Jordan." My resolve is beginning to fade as I look into his sad and doubtful eyes. He IS afraid for me. He really does care.

I take a deep breath and ask a question I am hoping will change my life. "Now, can you tell me which way is north?"

Chapter 6

I start the engine. It's running okay. I put the car in reverse and unsteadily back out of the tight space, trying to appear competent, but driving backward is hard. I vow to avoid it whenever possible. I swing out of the parking lot and drive slowly up the city street. Other cars are whizzing by me in the lane to my left. I sit as tall in the seat as I can. The gas is half full, so maybe I will have enough to get out of the city. So far, so good. I just need to focus and get the hang of this. I don't have time to be scared. My old life is fading in the rear view mirror—that's all I know. My fingers are numb from gripping the steering wheel so hard.

Miraculously, the city lights begin to fade behind me, and I begin to see signs to Wisconsin: Milwaukee, Green Bay beyond that. Another sign says the minimum speed is 60, so I watch the speedometer to make sure I'm going at least that fast. Even though it is the middle of the night, there are lots of other cars and gigantic trucks everywhere! I cringe as cars fly by me on the left, and trucks cruise past me slowly, penning me in. Miller's Fresh Food Transport is my savior—a trucker who drives along at a steady 55 to 60 through the flat, dark countryside. I stay a safe distance behind him and pray this truck with the big, red apples painted on the back will lead me safely through Milwaukee.

Those apples are hypnotizing, but my plan is working like a charm. When he slows down, I slow.

When he speeds up, I stay right behind him and feel almost invisible going along in his wake. We have reached the suburbs of Green Bay. I have been watching the gas gauge go down, and I only have a quarter tank. My eyes are twitching from the strain. I need to rest. A huge, lighted truck stop sign appears along the highway on my right, so I somehow manage to exit the highway in my zombie state. Turning toward the glow, I gratefully see a long row of gas pumps. I stop the car under a light pole at the far end of the lot to catch my breath and hear the engine cooling—tick, tick, tick—good ol' car. The place is quiet enough that a bored employee might wonder why a teenager is there so early in the morning by herself. I don't need to answer questions, but I do need sleep. I make sure all the doors are locked, recline the seat, pull up my comforter, and await the dawn.

The car clock says 10:00 am when I steer carefully up to the gas pump. I've never pumped gas before, but I read the little screen. The instructions tell me I have to pay cash before I put in gas, so this is my first test, and I prepare to lie again. *You can do this, Jenna.* It's a clean and almost painfully well-lighted place. I stride up to the counter and get in line with two twenty dollar bills. Doing a little math back at the pump, I figured that will buy me about fifteen gallons. I have no idea how much the car will hold, but I don't want to look totally clueless in here. The attendant, who is selling coffee to a long line of men and women on their way to work and trying to text someone at the same time, looks up at me.

"What pump?" she demands. I don't know the answer, so I hesitate and am holding up the line. A bearded man behind me overhears my predicament, leans toward me and whispers, "Buick?" I nod. "Pump 4."

"Pump 4," I reply confidently. He waves to me as he heads out to his car.

Thanks, someone, for putting written directions on this pump. I am happy to hear the gas swooshing through the hose into the car. The pump abruptly stops at $40. I wrestle with the hose and hang it up with a clatter. The smell of gasoline on my hands is the sweet smell of success. I park the car by the building, use the bathroom, buy a humongous plastic mug of pop and get back on the road. My gas tank is full. That's a huge relief.

The day has turned sunny and bright. Deep green forest lines the road on both sides with only an occasional mailbox and driveway to a hidden house. I pull into Iron Mountain, Michigan, by late afternoon. My plan is working so far. A bag of flour, salt, oatmeal, shortening, a couple of Cokes, rice, beans, matches, bug repellent, bologna, energy bars, bread, a box of fake cheese, twelve small bottles of water, and three gallons of distilled water go into my little cart with wonky wheels at the local grocery. I'm getting looks, as a stranger in this little town, so I'm making this as speedy as this goofy cart will let me. There is one woman at the checkout, but, again, I luck out because she is laughing at something on her phone. Her only comment to me as I check out and pay for my groceries with cash is, "Camping, eh?"

"Yes, ma'am. I'm with my family heading to Escanaba to do some fishing."

"Well, good luck. Need bait? Got minnows in the back."

"We're OK, thanks." She turns back to her phone and begins to chuckle as I wheel my groceries out the door.

Chapter 7

There it is—the faded driftwood sign. My heart swells. I'm totally too tired to cry. Vines have overgrown the sign and it hangs all crooked. I can't believe my memory has led me straight here—to Loon Haven. As I turn onto the overgrown sandy road, the car dips, and I hear the bottom scrape over a couple of big rocks. It's a narrow two-track that only lets one car at a time slowly move along. If you meet someone head-on on a Michigan two-track, the bigger vehicle usually pulls off into the woods to let the smaller car pull by. Small branches screech along both sides of the car, and I steer slowly and carefully between some saplings that have grown up right next to the lane. Overhanging tree limbs part over my windshield. I'm driving through a tunnel of spring. Evening is coming on fast, and I switch on my headlights. I don't know what I will find in the old clearing surrounding the cabin, but it sure doesn't look like I'm going to run into any people way back here.

My headlights glint off shattered window glass in what used to be a well-kept cabin. I can't believe what I am seeing. The four short years since Uncle Bill's death and my last visit have devastated the place. A huge pine tree has toppled over in heavy winds and crushed most of the roof. Moths and mosquitoes flash in my headlights. What a mess!

I can't stand to look at this anymore. I am desperate for sleep after my driving marathon. I'm too tired to even get out of the car to pee, so I securely lock all the doors, crawl over into the back seat, pull my comforter up on this chilly night, and I am out like a light.

I awake, disoriented. Have I suddenly gone blind? There is nothing but pitch darkness around me. I really do have to pee now and thinking about it is making it torture. I sit up, unlock the back door by my feet, listen for as long as my bladder will let me, and finally scoot out into the chilly spring night. After the little car interior light switches off, I literally can't see my hand before my face, but I squat right there by the car and go. I stand, feeling relief, with one hand on the damp roof of the car to anchor myself in this black space, and memories begin flooding back. The sounds of the crickets—a distant owl calling *Who cooks for you? Who cooks for you all?*, the clean air, the fragrance of the pines. Water is lapping on the sandy shore of the pond.

If this pitch dark clearing in the deep woods weren't so familiar to my very bones, I would be scared to death, but there seems to be something left of the spirit of Uncle Bill protecting me. I climb back into the car, lock all the doors again, and snuggle into the warmth of my comforter.

I am awakened from a deep sleep by the shuffling of someone strong pushing against the car. OMG, OMG! The car is rocking! I pull the comforter over my head and wait—for a voice, for a window to break—for what I don't know. I lie still under the covers and try my best to disappear. *Go away! Please go away, whoever you are!*

Dawn is breaking, but I am afraid to move a muscle. I'm getting awfully hot under these covers, so I finally take a peek. The windows are fogged up from my breath and body heat, so I can't get a clear view, but I can't stay in the car hiding like a coward. It is time to face whatever lies ahead. I can handle it, I think.

I unlock the door at my feet and scoot out. Yuck! My first step is into a giant pile of smelly poo! So much for my pink tennis shoes. A bear has been nosing around the car! That's what was trying to get in. He probably caught a whiff of the snacks on the front seat. He will be gone now that it is daylight. I wipe my shoe on the dewy grass. Gross!

In front of me is the cabin, or what is left of it, and beyond is my beloved pond, glistening and sparkling in the morning sun and drawing my steps like a magnet. It's just as I have remembered it a million times in my mind's eye—a small pond, ringed with brown cattails and white-barked birch trees. There is still a bit of winter on the pond: a ring of ice along the sandy shore. Leaves are stuck in the ice, creating a beautiful pattern of browns and clear bubbles. Chickadees are flitting in the underbrush calling their spring song. *Chicka dee dee dee, chicka dee dee dee* sweetly fills the air. The little black, white and gray birds are not very fearful of me and eye me curiously. I remember all the time Uncle Bill and I spent in the canoe paddling, listening, and watching the world surrounding us. He whispered the names of the different birds, plants, and animals, and, in the whispering, the names burrowed into my memory so much better than the loud teacher voices from in front of the blackboard in school. This is my real school of life, here in the north woods. He used to quote some things from a book he liked. I forget what it is now, but it was all about living life alone, but not lonely. He used to impress that on me. That you could be alone, but not lonely. I will have to think about that again now that I am here. I'm here!

I turn to look at the cabin. Reluctantly. Perhaps the damage isn't as bad as I thought in the dusk last night. Oh, boy. It's bad. Poor cabin. It's time to explore the place, though. If I'm going to hide out here for a while, I need to focus. Maybe there is something I can salvage out of this mess.

I part the branches of the fallen pine, sticky with spring sap, and search for the front door. At least this is where the front door used to be. The door has been knocked off the hinges, but, luckily, is still in one piece. Stooping, I gingerly creep into the cabin, testing my footing, because the floors are broken through in places. Luckily, three large limbs have formed a sort of tripod and seem to be securely holding the trunk and a portion of the roof up off the floor so I can finally stand up. To my right, the roof and the two bedroom loft have completely collapsed and are just a pile of rubble. Not much to salvage there except firewood. Under the loft was the kitchen area that used to have a small wooden table and four chairs—can't see 'em now. To my left, the stone chimney still stands, and the woodstove is covered by debris, but still on its legs. The floor is solid there.

Well, I know what I will be doing today. The job is before me. It's actually a relief to have some purpose, a plan. Just do it.

I decide to leave all the downed branches outside the cabin for now but begin to clear the loose branches out of the fireplace area. These lily white hands of mine are going to get a workout, so I grab Mom's winter knit gloves from the trunk. That's better. While I was out there getting the gloves, I realized the car could be easily seen from the air, so I took time to toss some branches onto the hood, top and trunk—camouflage. The idea of hiding out from the world for a while begins to turn from fear to a game like hide and seek. *Nyaah, nyaah, you can't find me.* Using new muscles and breaking a sweat feels good.

I work until I'm hungry. I'm pleased with my progress already. On the woodpile, I discover a rusty bow saw. Now, I can tackle the bigger branches. The huge trunk will just have to stay in place through the middle of the cabin, but it's not so hard to maneuver around now.

I take a break down by the lake with an apple and a bologna sandwich. Uncle Bill's favorite sandwich was thick slices of bologna slathered with bright yellow mustard on the cheapest, softest, white bread he could buy. He used to fix them for the two of us when we went fishing. I choked on the strong mustard the first time, but I wanted to copy everything he did, so it became my favorite summer sandwich, too.

I'm glad Uncle Bill's memory is here to keep me company. He is good company, and pleasant to think of. The things he taught me are building my confidence. I can feel it, even on this first day. When I go to rinse my hands in the pond, a dirty-faced girl with sticks in her hair grins up at me. I didn't know that my mouth and eyes remembered how to smile, but seeing my reflection releases even more of the pressure on my heart. A pair of loons are diving and surfacing on the far side of the pond, catching minnows, I suppose. I hope they will sing their eerie song for me at dusk tonight and stick around so I can watch them dive down and then guess where they will surface. Wish I had the old canoe right now, but wishes aren't getting me anywhere.

Evening finds me sore and scratched up. One branch has raked across my face and left a tender welt. I'm hungry again, but think I'll crawl in the car for a little nap.

I awaken to thunder and flashes of lightning. It is a fierce storm out there, and my little nap had turned into a mini-coma. I have no idea how long I have been asleep. The branches I threw over the car are swishing back and forth in the wind, probably not the best for the fine finish. I feel a bubble of a giggle rise up at that thought, the first joke I have made to myself in ages. I am holding myself lots more loosely already after one day of hard work and being responsible only for myself. I am beginning to realize how much effort it has taken over the past few years to be all wound up like a tight spring. What a relief to take deep breaths of air, though it is pretty stuffy in this car and the windows are all fogged up again. I lie back and listen as the storm passes overhead. Thunder is a mile away for each second you can count, Uncle Bill used to tell me, and we would sit on the cabin porch, listen, and count. I taught him to say *one hippopotamus, two hippopotamus* for the seconds and he laughed at that silliness. But when he timed me with his watch, counting hippos turned out to be really accurate, and he had to pay off his bet by being the one to dig the worms for the next day's fishing. I smile at the memory and count *one hippopotamus, two hippopotamus* under my breath. Lightning is four miles away over the pond to the south, according to four, fat hippos.

I can't sleep because of the storm, so I decide to plan. I've always liked to plan and see things through. Maybe that's another reason these last few years have been so rough. I never knew what the next hour would bring. I know that shelter is my first order of business. The car is a good safe shelter for now, but I can do better. I will need a screened in space to sleep out of the mosquitoes but where the summer breezes can keep me cool and comfortable. I am in the super dark again, so I might as well get more sleep. Work again tomorrow. My dwindling food supplies have me worried, but nothing I can do about that now. I'll figure something out. Live in the moment. I recall my uncle announcing to the family when I got too bossy, "Jenna is large and in charge." Well, I think maybe he was right. I have to use that to my advantage.

Chapter 8

Day dawns clear and sunny, so I grab an energy bar and a bottle of water and stroll around surveying what I accomplished on my first day home. Home, my home. It is good that the remaining roof shelters the woodstove area. The cot mattress is water and critter damaged, but the wooden cot frame is unbroken.

A divot in the flooring catches my eye. OMG! The root cellar! I had forgotten about it because it was forbidden territory when I was small. Uncle Bill would emerge carrying jars of sauerkraut and dried beans up the rickety ladder and through the trapdoor. His head would look funny coming up out of the hole in the floor, shoulders next, and strong arms carefully lifting the basket used to transport items up and down the ladder. The fewer the trips down there the better. Potatoes, carrots, and beets from the garden arose from its mysterious depths. I want to check it out, but first I have to cut and wrestle with a large limb resting heavily on the trapdoor. Using this little saw is like digging a ditch with a spoon. It's a whole morning's work.

Just. One. More. Limb. Whew! I slowly lift the hinged wooden door. Cool air wafts up from below as I kneel and peer into the depths. It is super dark down there, and spider webs cling to every surface, but the ladder is still in place and feels sturdy enough. I will sit here for a minute just to make sure I don't hear any critters stirring around down there. Sure don't want to run into a bunch of snakes or step onto something big and furry! My eyes begin to adjust as I count down seven ladder rungs and step off onto the dirt floor. I smell mushrooms, mold, and dirt. It is like air conditioning down here, and a shiver of both cold and excitement raises the hairs on my arms.

Yay! I have found a treasure trove! The sun sends a narrow beam through the demolished cabin roof all the way down onto the floor. One shelf holds candles, matches, a lantern and fuel, and water purification tablets. Uncle Bill's fishing gear is leaning in the corner: several rods, artificial lures and hooks in a small tackle box, a fishing net. There is a shelf with old, moldy-looking canned goods. Yucky, but the jars might be useful. A top shelf holds a couple of old books and the stained and well-used iron skillet cookbook inside the heavy, black skillet itself.

I stand and gaze around at it all and am transported back to a history class trip to the Field Museum just last fall. We had been studying Egypt, and the huge museum has a collection of mummies and some things from King Tut's tomb. The guide told us that when the man who discovered King Tut's tomb walked into all that treasure, he was so excited he tore off all his clothes, yelled "Eureka!", and danced around in the nude. It was the only time I ever heard my history class laugh as a whole—real laughter at something funny instead of laughing to cause pain to a teacher or a classmate. It made our whole group feel good about one another for a little while at least. Until we got on the bus to go back and the bullying began again. There was a little time, though, that was as awesome as the gold on the bracelets and rings in front of us. Why can't we humans just get along?

As I smile at that memory, I reach out and touch all the shelves in turn, going around and around soaking it all in. I'm not going to tear off my clothes, and this cellar is a little small for dancing, but I get it. I totally get it. Eureka! My new life begins here. *Thank you, Uncle Bill.*

It's creepy to thrust my hands into the shadowy corners, what with the spiders and all, but I'm excited to find more useful stuff. The metal shelves hold my weight, and I discover a small ventilation window up above one of the shelves making this space a perfect safe room. Lots safer than the car. If I climb down here, shut the trapdoor and throw the bolt inside, no one could know I was here or get to me. If someone did start to pry open the door above my head to do me harm, I can climb the shelves, squeeze through the vent, scramble on elbows and knees through the shallow crawl space under the cabin, and escape to safety in the woods. It's a good plan.

An old trunk is shoved under the shelves. The fragrances of old wool, pipe tobacco, and mothballs come flooding out. The memories flood out, too. Uncle Bill's fall and winter clothes are stored here, and there isn't any sign of damage. His Stormy Kromer cap of gray wool with ear flaps, a jacket fit for a lumberjack, heavy mittens that Uncle Bill called choppers, flannel-lined jeans, three pairs of warm socks, and three plaid flannel shirts useful in every season in the UP. I pull on one of the shirts to take the chill off, and, maybe it's my imagination, but I swear I can smell Uncle Bill's bay rum aftershave. He wasn't a big guy, and my arms are so long, I only have to turn up the sleeves one time to get a pretty good fit. The hat fits, too, and I feel honored to wear it. He thought a lot of this Michigan-made, traditional UP hat that my mom and I bought him for Christmas long ago. The bottom of the trunk has winter boots, unfortunately way too big.

I draw back my hand when I see a rifle and a box of ammunition. Whoa! Guns scare me. The guns I have seen the last few years were all aimed at people in anger and fear. The results sometimes stained the sidewalks on my way to school. I repack the clothing quickly and slam the trunk shut. Get that gun out of my sight.

What's in that leather case? It's hooked onto a canvas belt. Oh, yeah, it's the long, slender fillet knife used for cleaning fish and cutting the flesh from the bones. I pull it carefully from the sheaf. The knife still looks like new: clean, shiny, and ultra-sharp. I was never allowed to touch it as a kid. The pointed end looks deadly. It won't hurt to have this thing handy, so I put it back in the sheath and fasten the belt around my waist. This might afford me some protection, if I need it. At least, it will look impressive if I wave it around. I'm not sure if I could actually cut someone or something with it to protect myself, but it makes me feel like I could if it came to that.

I struggle up the ladder with the iron skillet. It weighs a ton. I go back down and retrieve the spinning rod and reel and a bass lure. I'm hungry for a hot meal. Can I do it? Won't know until I try.

I wipe the dust off the rod and reel and tie on the lure. Uncle Bill taught me a proper knot, but, shoot, I can't remember it now, so a regular shoelace knot will have to do. I approach the pond slowly and cast out toward the middle, away from the icy margin. Cast, retrieve. Cast, retrieve with a little jerky motion to set the lure in action. The lure is supposed to look like a wounded minnow to attract big fish. Maybe the water is too cold for fishing. Cast, retrieve. Over and over I watch the lure plop down in the water, line trailing after. I let it sit on the surface for a count of three hippopotamuses and then reel it in. Just as my mind is beginning to wander back toward all the work I have to do to get the cabin to serve as shelter, wham! The water explodes. "Fish on!" I loudly call out to no one but the trees. That's how I was taught to alert fellow fishermen to get their lines out of the way, and those words always caused everyone to take notice and join in the fun. The fish is pulling line and making the reel whiz. The rod bends and I can hear Bill's advice. *Hold the tip high, set the rod, keep even pressure, reel slowly. Let it run and play it. Good, Jenna. You're a champ.* The fish fights like a tiger. When I pull it in, it's not very big, but it is gorgeous. A beautiful, dark green bass that gave all his might to fight for his life. Maybe I should unhook him and let him go back in the water, but I am hungrier than I am merciful. I whack him on the head with the butt of the fillet knife to stun him out of his misery and toss him on the wet grass next to me just the way Uncle Bill taught me. His scales glisten and his gills open and close even in death. I cast out again, and, after a dozen casts, I have two more little bass. Perfect for shore lunch.

My stomach is growling in anticipation of a hot meal. I set about gathering some small branches from the yard. I clear leaves out of the old campfire pit and use the matches to get a fire going in dry pine needles first, then larger and larger wood until there is a little bed of coals. I behead, clean out the guts of the three fish, and scale them with my knife. They don't look too bad even if I have mauled them a little. They sizzle as they hit the hot shortening in the iron skillet. Oh, boy. Sliding them onto a flat stone, I let them cool until I can hold the first one in my fingers and nibble carefully at the tender flesh leaving the skeleton behind. Yum! These little fellows only provide a tiny taste—and they are a little burned—but the flavor is absolutely wonderful. I did it! Another time, I will catch more to actually fill me up and maybe fix some beans or rice, too. But for now it is just good that I can figure out how not to starve for as long as I am hiding out here. Again, I remind myself to focus and take it one day at a time.

Returning to the cabin, I pull an old broom from under the rubble, and sweep the leaves and pinecones down the steps toward the lake. Looking to my left, I had almost forgotten the little screened-in back porch, but I get on my knees and peek through downed branches. The porch is still standing! This small space is a safe place to sleep because I remember helping Uncle Bill reinforce the screen and the wood with wire hardware cloth to discourage the bears and the porcupines. It has kept them out and from gnawing the wood, as porcupines will do. I will be fine sleeping there as long as I don't bring any food into that area. That is what bears are really after—not to eat me. I hope. My afternoon project will be to set up a new bedroom out of the car and into the house. Wow! This is a milestone, and I celebrate by eating the last apple and drinking the last Coke for a snack while gazing at the pond. The loons are still there, diving and popping up through the sparkling water. I watch one maneuver a minnow into his beak and stretch out his neck to give a great swallow. Down the hatch! *You and I will have to share the fish in this pond, Mr. Loon.*

I cut away the branches around the porch and push aside the squeaky screen door. The old wooden rocking chair is there and the glider couch where we used to sit when the mosquitoes got bad. Uncle Bill didn't smoke his pipe in the cabin, but he would fire it up out here. Fragrant wafts of smoke. I would pretend to object and choke, but secretly I loved the smell of his pipe. The ritual of lighting it was a fascinating part of his identity to a little girl. An old pipe is in the ashtray just as he had left it four years ago: the last time he sat on this porch before his death. I pick it up and sniff the stale tobacco. I'll leave it right there to remind me of him and give me the feeling that he is just out fishing or in the next room. I sweep the mouse droppings off the floor and go out to the car to bring in a few things.

The porch only has screens, no glass windows, so the rain and wind will get in. I decide to pitch my tent on the floor. That will give me an extra layer of protection against rain, mosquitoes, and cool nights. Brilliant! The tent just pops up—no stakes required. I air out the blankets and sleeping bag and my pink comforter for a couple of hours, until the funky old car smell is gone, and layer them in the tent floor. I'm going to be as snug as a bug in a rug, as Mom used to say. I take a moment to admire and to straighten a neatly framed woodcut print with a saying by a fellow named Henry David Thoreau, something about birds.

If I am going to be here for a while, I also have to think about finding the old outhouse. I can't continue to pee and poop in the woods, like my friend the bear. The old "facility," as Uncle Bill called it, is down a grassy trail at the edge of the woods. My grandfather had built it many years before I was born. He decided he wanted an open view of the pond while he was sitting on the toilet, so he built it with just three sides. Using the open air outhouse was always pretty awkward. We solved the embarrassment by first stopping at a little birdhouse-like structure that held toilet paper. When you had to use the toilet, you would tear off a couple of pieces of paper and holler, "Comin'on!" If there was no answering shout, "Occupied," it was safe to proceed. I smile at the remembrance. A funny little family ritual all our own.

I retrace the path and, sure enough, there is the toilet paper box. Squirrels have shredded the paper, but the old cedar outhouse is still there. It is full of leaves, pinecones, and needles, but the roof is still intact and the seat lid okay. The scenic view is sure still there. A little work with the broom and I will be back in business…for me to do my business. Another joke. I'm cracking myself up here. I've even got a partial roll of toilet paper in the car to last me a while. I get it and install it in the box, just for the sake of tradition.

I'm ready to take a break from cleaning. The day is lovely and the pond so beautiful. The storm bought warm air from the south. The first mayflies are flitting up and down over the pond. Uncle Bill once showed me how the mayfly larvae climb up out of the water, split their skins and take wing. Dragonflies and mosquitoes do that, too, even though it seems weird that some bugs live part of their lives under water. Sunfish and bass kiss the surface and leave behind ever widening ripples. Blue sky is reflected on the water. Water lilies are beginning to reach the surface, and the turtles are coming out of their winter sleep. Their little heads cruise along in the search for food. I think they hide down in the mud during the winter and breathe through their skin, somehow. Maybe there is something about that in one of the books in the root cellar. I'll look later.

I grab my fishing pole and walk the trail to the far side of the pond. The path is overgrown with berry brambles that are a nuisance now, but will be great to pick and eat in August. August? What am I thinking? *Day by day, Jenna, day by day.*

Under a couple rocks, I find three nice worms. Rigging my line with a hook, sinker, and round red and white bobber, I string a worm on the hook and toss it out toward the middle. The fish are hungry. Before long, I have four sunfish and a perch lying on the grass next to me. I clean them and toss the heads and guts under a struggling wild rose in my front yard, wrap the fish in wet leaves and carry them to the fire pit. Think I will try to get sort of fancy for dinner tonight, as my stomach feels a pinch from the lack of solid food from the last few days. I build a nice fire and set my big skillet on the coals. I get the bag of rice and a gallon of water from the trunk, along with a spoon and fork, and pour some rice in the skillet along with about three cups of water. The ratio is three to one—learned that in the lame class the high school called Culinary Arts, another name for Problem Teens with Permission to Handle Sharp Knives. I put plenty of salt in there, too, because I have a huge craving for it after my fast food diet of the past month. An old leather glove from off the woodpile makes a good hot pad. The rice simmers, then boils. I hold the pan up to get it to cook slowly, but the heavy pan is about to break my wrists. Up and down, up and down, off the heat, on the heat, stoke the fire, stir, smoke in my eyes. This is a workout. After the rice seems pretty well cooked, I broil my fish on sticks over the coals. They are a little charred, and one falls off into the fire setting up a billow of smoke and flame, but I use my fingers to flake the flesh off the bones and over the rice. I end up with a huge dinner. It's definitely too salty, and the rice is tough. My meal tastes as much like wood smoke as I smell on my clothes and hair, but it is the best food I have ever had in my life! Every forkful is warm and comforting, and I eat slowly, chewing the tough rice, but enjoying every bite. A kingfisher perched in a dead branch over the water chatters and scolds. I think he is congratulating me on being a good fisherman—fisherwoman—fisherperson. How about just fisher? I smile and watch him dive headfirst into the water and come up, glistening minnow in his beak. He alights on the snag and tosses the fish around until it goes down with a big gulp. He actually has a big lump in his neck where that live fish has to still be wriggling around. Glad I can chew. "See, Mr. Kingfisher, there are enough fish in this pond for the two of us and Mr. Loon, too." I realize I have said this aloud. *Man, oh, man. Now I am talking to the ghost of Uncle Bill, myself, and animals. This is getting sort of like a weird Disney movie.*

For a moment, I flash back in time to cruel Sheila. I know her memory shouldn't get to me, but you can be shoved, slapped, insulted, and demeaned just so long until you either react violently, or you buy into the idea you somehow deserve that treatment because your clothes don't fit, you live in a car, your mom is a drug abuser, your hair is not styled, you don't have a cell phone or fake fingernails, shiny lips or fancy eye shadow. Sheila wouldn't have survived an hour here. Can you envision her stepping in bear poo? I have to laugh when I picture Sheila hopping around on one foot and putting up a howl that would have been heard a mile away. What a helpless mess she would be when the nights get black as pitch and the mosquitoes buzz around her head. Well, let her rot in the city. She will have to find someone else to bully. This girl is meant for the woods, not the suburbs or the mean city streets.

My eyes are red and irritated from the wood smoke, and, gotta admit, even a little teary from some of my leftover anger at Sheila. Bringing up my sleeve to dry my tears, I catch a whiff of my flannel shirt. Phew! Gosh! Even though I am a woods girl now, I don't have to look like a mossy turtle or smell like a badger! I haven't even done as much as wash my face or brush my teeth for nearly a week! Traditionally at the cabin, baths were taken in the lake with a bar of soap, but the last bits of ice are still crowding along the shores—way too cold for swimming. I find a black trash bag under the passenger's seat of the car, fill it with a couple of gallons of lake water, and hang it on a hook against the south wall of the cabin. Uncle Bill once taught me this solar invention.

After a couple more hours of work in the cabin, I return to the bag, which feels nicely lukewarm from the sun. I take it down and carry it to a hollow stump, gently lowering the bag to form a sink full of warm water. It feels funny to be taking off all my clothes out here in the open, but I decide to pretend I'm in the girls' locker room at school. I get naked and wash with a washcloth and dish soap from the box in the trunk. I end up smelling like a lemon, but it beats B.O. and wood smoke. Last, I wash and rinse my hair. The warm water is a luxury. Ahhh. I feel so much better. I put together a warm, dorky outfit of clean underwear, jeans and socks topped by another of Uncle Bill's warm flannel shirts, plunge my dirty laundry in my makeshift sink to soak, and sit down by the pond and let the light breeze and sun dry my hair. When it is dry, I loosely braid it to keep it out of my way.

Tonight is a big night. I will sleep on the cabin porch instead of in the car. I'm a little scared because I am letting go of one layer of protection, but excited, too, because it is a huge step to shedding my old life and embracing the new one. I need to get ready before dark, so I climb down into the root cellar to bring up the lantern. I think I remember how to light it, but it is sort of tricky. While I am down there, I notice an old bird identification book and a beat up hard copy of *Walden* by that guy Thoreau. That's the one Uncle Bill liked. Might as well take that upstairs, too.

I carry the lantern and box of matches outside, fill the tank with smelly fuel and fiddle around with the knob and matches, almost scorching my eyebrows, until the lamp hisses and throws out a clear, bright light. I experiment with turning it up high and down low before turning the lantern off and watching the glow fade. The supply of white gas in the root cellar should last me a long time, but I better conserve it.

I actually put on pink pajamas that are way too small but make me feel like I'm totally going to bed for once instead of just passing out where I sit. The tent is snug. There is enough padding on the floor to be pretty comfortable, and all my familiar pillows and comforter surround me. I smell like a lemon drop and resolve to wash and air dry my bedding tomorrow. I will just shut my eyes for a moment.

Chapter 9

Laughter is coming from somewhere far, far away. Mom and Uncle Bill must be playing poker at the kitchen table. She is so lucky at cards. I'm sure she has a won a pile of quarters from him. I'll go in and see, but something is clutching at me, holding me fast. "Mom! Mom!" I churn my legs to get to her.

Another troubling dream. This one has left me shaken and sweaty. It all seemed so real. The laughter, the light. Then, the wild laughter rises again, out on the lake. It's the loons calling out in their joy at the light of the full moon rising over the pines and glistening in a line to the shore. My hammering heart slows as the full weight of my loss makes me ache all over. The two people I loved the most were right there at my fingertips—almost in my grasp. I could have hugged them both and held them fast, but they disappeared like the wood smoke of my campfire. I seldom even touched my mom in the last few years. So deeply disappointed and disgusted with her coughing, dirty and frail body, and her habit that cost us so much—cost me so much. It always is about me, isn't it? I hated the lying and the hard scrabble to stay warm and fed, but I sure wish I could hug her now. I wish she smelled like a lemon drop and was warmly tucked into her sleeping bag beside me here in this place she loved so much. We could talk about things that matter, and laugh, and I could tell her I love her. She could teach me to play poker.

Wishes, aching heart, hunger and the bright moon take away any chance for sleep. I sit up, my shoulder grazing the tent side, my comforter in a tangle. Looks like a pillow fight in here, and I'm thirsty, too, after all that tossing, turning, and running in my sleep.

Maybe I'll read a while. Reading almost always makes me drowsy, and this old ratty copy of *Walden* looks boring enough to put me to sleep. I wish I had a good romance, but this is better than nothing. After the vivid dream fades a bit, it is actually a gorgeous night. The moon is so bright it outshines the stars. Its path stretches silver before me as if one could just set out across the pond and walk straight up to the moon. Maybe that is where people go when they die. Maybe Mom and Uncle Bill walked hand in hand up that silver path and can come back to visit when the moon is full. No, I don't think that is it. Their presence is always here. At least I have felt Uncle Bill beside me, and now my young, vibrant mom has arrived, as well. It's a comforting thought I must hang on to. They are with me at their best and the memories are palpable. Uncle Bill is whistling as he shaves out by the lake in the mornings, mirror hanging on the tree. Mom dressed in her jeans and favorite sweatshirt, a smile on her face, making coffee and cooking fish and rice for dinner. Hers tasted lots better than mine, I must admit. And asparagus! Oh, yes, the asparagus that I picked out of the rice and laid on the edge of my plate. Too slimy for me cooked but yummy when snapped off fresh where it grows wild on the margins of the clearing. Tomorrow, I go hunting for the wild asparagus. *Hold on to us as we are in these memories, Jenna. We can remain forever just the way you picture us in this moment.* I can hear them as if they are on this porch with me. All is forgiven, and a great weight is lifted off my shoulders. When I crawl out from my tent, stand and take a deep breath of the night air, I feel as if I am floating.

The moonlight gives me just the right amount of light to fuss with the lantern. I manage to light it safely and set it to hissing and glowing with an intense, white light. Curling up in the rocking chair, my eyes are drawn to the bird print on the wall for the first time. Birds with flashes of red on their shoulders are winging over and through brown cattails. *The first sparrow of spring! The year beginning with younger hope than ever! The faint silvery warblings heard over the partially bare and moist fields from the bluebird, the song sparrow, and the red wing, as if the last flakes of winter tinkled as they fell! Henry David Thoreau.* I guess Henry thinks the new year starts with spring, when most people believe it to begin on cold, dreary January 1. I get what he's saying. This year has started for me in the spring, and I am beginning with hope that is sure young because I haven't felt hope for so long. The red wings are my neighbors. They have been swinging on and pecking the fluff from last year's cattails every evening when they gather on the far side of the pond to sleep at night. Bluebirds and sparrows may have soft voices like he says, but I have to disagree about the redwings. They put up an awful fuss: *warble-a-CHEE, warble-a-CHEE*!

The crickets are *cheep, cheeping.* An owl can be heard softly in the distance, and a brisk breeze is stirring the surface of the pond, sending the moon's reflection into a wobbly path. My eyes keep slamming shut. Closing the book, I extinguish the lamp and crawl back into the tent. Tomorrow is another day and another fresh start.

Chapter 10

Uncle Bill's spirit is so proud of me. I can feel it. I have cut fourteen notches on the board framing my front door, one for each day I have been here. The row of notches both amazes me and gives me a sense of pride. I carve a new one each morning as I go out to say hello to the pond and visit the outhouse. Fourteen busy days of work and fourteen evenings of reading and sound sleep. The nightmares are fewer, pleasant dreams more often, and I have fallen into a routine. I have gone a whole two weeks without the sound of a human voice other than my own, and I am not self-conscious any more about greeting the birds and other critters aloud. Reading *Walden* aloud at night seems to help me understand better.

I heard something long ago about a guy named Johnny Appleseed. The story said he wore a cooking pot as a hat and talked to everyone and everything that crossed his path. He was mostly trying to get them to believe in his unusual religious ideas. Well, I thought he sounded pretty weird, but I talk to animals now, and a cooking pot would make a pretty good rain hat. I cut a hole in a black plastic bag and pull it over my head and onto my shoulders when I have to use the outhouse on a rainy day. Makes a good poncho. So, who is laughing now? I think Uncle Bill is.

On this rainy day, I am sitting in my rocking chair thinking about the last week and what I got done around here. I had my first swim. Brrr. It was a quick dip in the frigid water, but it brought back lots of good memories along with the goosebumps. When I was here before, I wasn't tall enough to touch bottom. It was a shock today when my feet got tangled in weeds and sank in the mucky bottom. I squealed like a pig, and swam like a crazy woman to get on the sandy beach. Ick…ick! So gross.

I continued to cut and clear branches and wooden roof shingles from the demolished area of the cabin. This job entailed a lot of crawling around on the floor to make progress on all that mess. The broken shingles went on the woodpile. They will be good to burn later when I decide to try my luck with the woodstove. The thing scares me a bit because I sure don't want to burn the place down. As a kid, I was commanded to bring in loads of wood for the wood box, but I was forbidden to touch any part of the stove.

An inventory of treasures rescued from the rubble include: a tin of black pepper and some other herbs and spices I don't know what to do with, two unbroken chairs, three tin pie plates and cups, a cast iron cooking pot with lid, smashed table and two broken chairs only fit for the woodpile, silverware for six (as if I'm ever going to need that), a good spatula, cooking spoon, and, best of all, the contents of the junk drawer, which held a ball of string, duct tape, a pair of pliers, two screwdrivers that turn different kinds of screws, and a coffee can full of all sorts of nails and screws. I found a little bolt to screw to the inside of the screen door on the porch so I can lock myself in at night. Not much security, but it would slow down a two-legged or four-legged intruder until I could get prepared to either fight or to bowl them over and run.

I'm sprouting muscles for the first time in my life. Noticed my arms tanned and toned the other day. Sheila would get a surprise if she tried to shove me now. I'd deck her and watch her posse run!

The rose bramble is sending out one long shoot with a pink bud, my favorite. I am still tossing the leftovers from my fish cleaning into the middle of it. It's sort of fun to feed it as I feed myself. I'm not talking to it—yet.

Almost made a big mistake the other day. Now that I have run out of toilet paper, I decided I would have to use leaves, instead. I was in kind of a hurry and reached down to snag some leaves, when a rhyme alarmed in my head. *When the leaves are three, leave them be.* OMG, I almost used poison ivy. It's sort of funny to think of it now, but that sort of carelessness could have cost me my freedom here. I have to protect my freedom at all costs, so *get your head in the game, Jenna, and keep your edge.* I hear you, Uncle Bill.

I'm building an early cooking fire today because my menu of fish on a stick, fish and rice, fish with melted Velveeta, rice and Velveeta, and plain rice is getting more boring than the free lunches at school. I'm going to try to cook dry beans, and I know it takes a long time. I put water and beans in my newly discovered pot over the coals. I think I can just check on them once in a while and add a little wood and water to keep things bubbling along. I'm going to skip fishing today and spend some time doing a sketch of the cabin the way I remember it as a kid, not squashed by a tree. I gather the pens I lifted from the free clinic every time I would take Mom there. A big spiral-bound sketchbook was given to me by my art teacher, Mr. D. I had almost forgotten about it but found it shoved under the driver's seat of the car. The paper is large and thick, perfect for drawing. Using a pen to draw is sort of frustrating because I can't erase anything, but that forces me to pay closer attention. Mr. D was a cool guy I liked, and the other students liked him, too. His classroom was a safe place to be. He taught us to train our eye by drawing something by always keeping our eyes on the subject and not looking at or lifting the pen from the paper. I try to get my hand to follow the path of my eyes as I study the lines of the old leaning outhouse. My drawing turns out looking pretty funny, but the outhouse is sort of funny-looking anyway. I shade it in with different styles of crosshatching like Mr. D taught me, and create shadows with a piece of charred wood I fished from the edges of the campfire.

Pulling up my knees and hugging them with my arms, I relax and get lost in dreams. It is fun to remember the old cabin as it was when I was little: the dark porch and evenings on the glider with the fragrance of Uncle Bill's pipe and murmur of quiet conversation. The kitchen counter was often piled with vegetables from the garden, and the table would have colorful wildflowers in a canning jar. The famous pig cookie jar was always full. The cot was neatly made up with a granny square afghan and a soft down pillow covered by blue and white ticking. A blue and white braided rug covered the root cellar door. Uncle Bill's bedroom was in the loft, accessed by a ladder that pulled down from the ceiling into the middle of the living room. I was not allowed to climb the ladder. His room was off limits. There was another small bedroom up there that he used as a closet. Under the loft was the kitchen and one tiny bedroom. In the summers, I loved to stay in my downstairs room with the twin beds and cozy, flowered coverlets.

My thoughts wander to something I read the other night in *Walden*. A lot of that book is sort of over my head. I think it is mostly made up of ideas instead of a story about the outdoors. I thought it was going to be Henry's adventures living on a pond like I am, but the ideas seem lots bigger than that. I know how and why I ended up here by myself, but I couldn't figure out why he just walked outside of his town a few miles and built a cabin—sort of like camping in the backyard. But then I read: *I went to the woods because I wished to live deliberately, to front only the essential facts of life, and see if I could not learn what it had to teach, and not, when I came to die, discover that I had not lived.* I've been thinking about that for a couple of days and even have this sentence memorized. I started by trying to figure out what deliberately meant. I remember hearing a teacher say, "You deliberately knocked Jenna's books to the floor. It wasn't an accident." So, deliberately means you know exactly what you are doing. Henry is saying he wants to live by knowing exactly what he is doing, instead of just going along with everyone else without thinking. I wasn't living deliberately in Chicago. Mom and I were living like scared victims. Here, I have a purpose for everything I do, and to not only survive, but to make a good life. Already I am happier and healthier. I eat, sleep, wake up and just do life every day. I have a purpose. Henry wasn't just loafing around on his pond, he was really thinking about himself and his life. Being out alone makes you do that. He describes a lot of animal and plant life around his pond, and I skip over some of that because it gets boring, but I like the parts in his book where he thinks about his own life. I'm going to keep reading. Henry is good company.

I silence the hiss and glow of the lantern on my fourteenth night. My tent is comfortable and, after a busy day around this place, I always fall asleep right away. Sometimes I awaken in the middle of the night to some sort of sound around the cabin. The coyotes pass between the cabin and the pond often in search of mice, rabbits, and ground nesting birds. A kill sends up a bloodcurdling *Yip Yippee!* from the whole pack and was really scary the first time I heard them, but I am safe from them in here. Ahh, this sleeping bag feels great.

I am torn from pleasant dreams by something walking right next to my tent. Instantly I am on high alert and grab for my knife belt. It's just dawn and something is trying to get into the porch. A large shadow passes by, and I hear scratching on the screen. I unsheathe my knife, slowly get my legs out of the bag so I can be ready to run, and freeze in place, waiting and hoping whatever it is will go away. It could be the bear—about the right size. I don't hear breathing, but there is definitely shuffling in the leaves as something or someone moves around out there. I decide to go on the offensive. *Make yourself large and in charge, Jenna.* I need to force whatever it is to hightail it as fast as it can. So, I crouch ready to explode onto the porch waving my arms, hollering, and brandishing my weapon.

Now's the time to make my move! I lunge out of the tent yelling at the top of my lungs, "Whoever you are, get out of here before I kill you!"

I am astonished by the face of a grizzled man peering through the screen at me. He has long, wild hair, a stained canvas jacket, and round glasses. His hands are holding something, his mouth wide open in surprise. I scream and race for the root cellar door. Behind me comes a deep shout of fear and the sound of awkward footfalls, like a drunken man running. I pull down the trap door on my way down, latch it securely, and hit the dirt floor with a thud. It's pitch black in here. Curled in a corner, arms hugging my knees, I sob with surprise, shock and foreboding. I muffle my sobs into my bent knees. I must be quiet so he goes far, far away where I will never see him again. My world has just been invaded. I am violated.

After what seems to be an eternity of silence, I fumble around and find a votive candle to shed a little light on my confinement. I am going to stay here for hours, not only out of fear but thoughts about my future here, if I even have one now I have been discovered. After the adrenaline wears off a bit, I realize I have known all along that it was very likely my hiding place would be found out and my life of purpose destroyed. How stupid to think there would never be a hunter, fisherman, or even the rightful owner of the property show up to claim it or to report me to the cops. Is all my hard work for nothing? Am I in as much danger here as I was in the city? I have been fooling myself playing house here in the woods. How can Loon Haven break my heart like this?

I finally climb out of my hole, carefully scanning the area all around the cabin and the lakeshore. No sign of anyone except for some boot prints in the sandy beach. I decide to move my bedding to the root cellar. I will sleep down there locked in for a while and wear my knife 24/7.

Chapter 11

My 21st notch today—no sign of the trespasser for a whole week, but it creeps me out to know someone is aware of where I am and could be watching me, or, even worse, going to the cops to report a teenager alone and in the woods. Running away from here will not solve anything; I have nowhere to go. I do not want to leave the spirits of Uncle Bill and Mom behind. They will help to protect me. *Please. Please.*

Each passing day boosts my confidence, and I have slowly gone back to my routine. I'm really powerless to do anything else. My trips to the waterfall that feeds the pond are getting to be habit; the path through the ferns is worn by my trips back and forth to fill my water jugs. The tea-colored water streaming over and swirling around the flat stones is fresher, colder, and better tasting than the water from the pond, and I have decided I would rather drink water that hasn't had turtles lounging in it. The purification tablets make the water taste metallic but sure beats having gross parasites running around my insides and making me sick.

This plastic jug is slowly filling under the cascading water. OMG. Suddenly, I feel the hairs on the back of my neck prickle and my shoulders tense up. No strange noises, but my instincts kick in, and I know I'm not alone. A deep voice makes me jump. He's very close. I may get hurt, here, but my knife blade glints in my hand and I'm not only scared, I'm angry.

"Hey, kid."

I jump up, wave my knife, and put my back up against a big maple tree. "Don't come near me or I swear I will kill you."

"Geez, kid, take it easy, eh."

I shout in as loud and deep a voice as I can manage. "This property belongs to my grandfather. He and my uncle will be here soon with their guns, and you will be sorry you messed with me."

"I'm not trying to mess with you. Just listen a sec." He steps from behind a tree into view.

"No! Get outta here!" I point my knife at his chest and take a couple steps forward, but he does not back off.

"Just quit with the bull," he bellows. "I knew your granddad. He's dead. Your uncle was my best friend. He's dead, too. Calm down and let me talk to you a minute, eh." His voice softens, "I'm sorry we scared each other the other day. I just figured out who you are."

"What do ya mean? You don't know me."

"You're Bill's niece, right?"

I draw back and look him over. He doesn't seem to have a weapon on him, thank God. His sandy hair is pulled back in a short ponytail and he has on regular jeans and a red and black plaid shirt under a tan fishing vest. He is carrying a long fly rod. The only thing that resembles the scary guy staring at me through the porch screen is the round glasses. He's not an old man like I thought before—maybe my mom's age.

Stay aggressive. Protect yourself. You don't know this guy. "I don't know what you are talking about. I own this property and you are trespassing. Get off it!" I yell at the top of my lungs. I'm as close to him as I dare to get.

He raises his hands up, palms out, in an attitude of surrender, his fishing rod dangling by his right thumb. "Okay, okay. I'm going, I'm going. Just so's you know, I'm not going to report you as a squatter. What you do is your own business. Just sorry you are so danged unsociable, but I guess you must have your reasons. You don't have to worry about me. I'll stay away from you, but you may run into me. I'm your closest neighbor out here."

He turns and walks away down the trail. His shoulders are slumped, and he has a bad limp. I definitely could outrun this guy. I have made him back down! He startles me by sadly adding without looking back, "Name's Skip."

Chapter 12

Thirty-one days! I've been here a whole month. The days are so long now I sleep late in the morning, drink a big glass of water to quell my hunger, work for a couple of hours at camp chores, eat a big middle of the day meal of beans and rice, hike around the lake with my sketch pad in hand, and snack on fried fish cooked over my evening campfires before reading and bed. It's my own schedule and it suits me. Keeping up with the new developments on the pond and in the woods has sharpened my eyes and ears. The loons have little ones now. The chicks ride on their mother's back as she swims around! It's so cute. I'm catching more big bass as the water warms up. Swimming is really fun, and I have conquered any fear of cruising with the muskrats and turtles, who seem to accept me as any other creature of the woods and water. Even got brave enough to touch bottom yesterday. It was squishy, but nothing bit me.

The wild rose bush is blooming with one single pink flower. It loves my fish fertilizer.

My dwindling food supply concerns me. I have used three quarters of my big bags of rice and beans, and that's about all that is left. The canned goods in the cellar looked yucky, so decided to dump all the jars. Not worth taking a chance of poisoning myself. I've made some tasty meals of raw wild asparagus and cooked morel mushrooms. To get more supplies, I may have to see if the car will start and drive into the village of Birch Bay to the grocery there, but I know I will attract lots of attention and gossip if I do because up here everyone is in everyone else's business and they are either related to one another or have known each other forever. I might be able to pull off acting like a camper from the municipal campground on the lake. I've still got over $100 squirreled away in the upholstery. I have decided to wait until it is absolutely necessary to make an appearance in the outside world.

It is a glorious evening. The breeze is just enough to keep down the mosquitoes and the pesky black flies have pretty well run their course in the last few weeks. One day last week, I spent from sunrise to sunset reading and sketching on the porch because on my trips to the outhouse those nasty bugs dive-bombed my nose, mouth, eyes, the part on my scalp, the creases in my elbows and around my neck. They bite as soon as they land and raise a big, itchy, painful welt. The Deet I bought doesn't help at all. Wish I had a head net. I found the remains of one in a big mouse nest in the woodpile. Tonight, though, the bugs have let up some, and so I build a nice fire, sit back and watch as the smoke travels in a wispy stream out over the lake.

"You are attractin' lots of attention with that smoky fire." The voice startles me. The words are far off and hard to make out, but I recognize the deep voice.

"Stop stalking me! I'm going to call the cops. I have my cell phone right here!"

"Yeah, right, kid. Not stalkin'—just walkin'."
Then a chuckle and *swish, thump, swish, thump* moving away from me.

"You are a jerk! Get outta here!"

What a way to ruin a good evening, but, so far, he has been good for his word about not turning me in. I gotta keep on the alert, though. Of all the hazards in this woods, including the bears and the poison ivy, he is the only thing threatening my freedom. *Keep your focus, Jenna—right, Uncle Bill? Right, Uncle Bill?* For the first time, I don't feel his guidance. I'm going to have to deal with this myself.

I don't run to the root cellar this time. I'm standing my ground and going to enjoy this campfire on this beautiful evening. In the distance I hear pops and explosions. What could be going on? The sound is coming from my left—a number of miles away. Sounds like a war going on in Birch Bay. It's not hunting season. Wonder what's up? Oh, gosh—fireworks! That's it. It must be the 4th of July. That's cool. I love fireworks because—my breath catches. Oh, man. Today is my birthday, and Uncle Bill always set a few bottle rockets off over the lake just for me every year. A chill runs over me, and a great wave of sadness and loss. None of those people are here to give me a special day: no cake, no sweet icing and candles to blow out, no fireworks, no gifts wrapped up with ribbon. I'm not here with new friends or a boyfriend, or anyone to wish me a happy birthday. Happy birthday, hell. It's an unhappy birthday, for sure.

I'm tired but not sleepy. Henry has a chapter in his book called "Solitude," and I turn to it to see what he might say about how bummed I am tonight.

I love to be alone….We are for the most part more lonely when we go abroad among men than when we stay in our chambers....We meet at very short intervals, not having had time to acquire any new value for each other….We have had to agree on a certain set of rules, called etiquette and politeness, to make this frequent meeting tolerable, and that we need not come to open war….We live thick and are in each other's way, and stumble over one another, and I think that we thus lose some respect for one another….I am no more lonely than the loon in the pond that laughs so loud, or than Walden Pond itself.

Leaning my head back and closing my eyes, I decide he is right. I felt lonelier surrounded by tens of thousands of people in Chicago than I feel here. I was in other people's way there, and they were in mine. We stumbled over each other, and I never took the chance to get to know anyone well. Mr. D. probably wasn't the only good teacher, and my generous friend Jordan was totally worth knowing better. I knew my mother well, but over time she wasn't the same person. We became strangers to one another, and, I couldn't tell where love left off and duty took over—a loneliness that was confusing and made my heart ache. I have been afraid here by myself from time to time when the unexpected has happened, but I am comfortable by myself: alone but not lonely.

Chapter 13

This Skip guy is really creeping me out. Every evening it is the same old thing. No sooner than I build my campfire to fry my fish snack and sit down to cook on my nice coals, I hear the uneven footfalls going through the ferns in the woods on the other side of the pond. *Swish, thump, swish, thump.* He heads east to west first, and always has something to say, "Hey, kid. Gonna rain tomorrow—feel it in my bones—get ready, eh. Hey, kid, a shiny spoon lure with a treble hook really worked for me. Latched onto a muskie today and will have two dinners from him. Hey, kid, how's your woodpile comin'? It will be winter before you know it. Hey, kid, weather is right for the northern lights." I sit and silently steam—it's a waste of breath for this "kid" to yell back. Always, on his return trip west to east he loudly exclaims, "Not stalkin', just walkin',"and then he lets out an infuriating deep chuckle. He thinks he is sure clever, that stupid, stupid guy.

My root cellar hideout stands open and ready for me in case he gets too close. I know I can outrun him with that bad leg of his. It helps if I pretend he is just another animal out there, a groundhog. Henry cooked and ate a groundhog that was eating the beans in his garden. He didn't like either killing or eating it, so he went back to his vegetarian diet.

If I learn to use the woodstove in the cabin for cooking, I can get out of his sight in the evenings. He should leave me alone, 'cause that's what I want to be:

alone. It doesn't get dark until ten thirty this time of year, so I have plenty of time to gather some small, dry sticks and get that thing going after work. I wish I had paid more attention when Uncle Bill and mom ran that stove, but it can't be any big deal. Just look at all the stuff I have figured out myself. I know Henry would be proud. Skip's comment about winter coming has me thinking. I've been living day by day for so long, I sort of forgot about next month and the month after that. Time to put my copy of *Walden* aside and think about how I will stay warm and feed myself.

Henry writes a lot about shelter in his book. He built a snug little house really cheap on his pond and did a lot of bragging about it. I guess I would brag, too, if I built a whole house for less than $30, but, actually, I have a pretty awesome house already. It just is really, really open to the elements, to say the least. I sweep out wet pine needles and chase out the red squirrels most mornings. This place is my shelter and also my responsibility for as long as my luck holds out. Henry thinks you should read to figure out how to do everything for yourself—to be self-reliant. I have a feather stuck in the book on one of my favorite pages, turn to it, and read aloud:

"Which would have advanced the most at the end of the month,--the boy who had made his own jackknife from the ore which he had dug and smelted, reading as much as would be necessary for this, -- or the boy who had attended the lectures on metallurgy at the Institute in the mean while, and had received a Rogers' penknife from his father? Which would be most

likely to cut his fingers?" Henry thinks he's pretty clever, but he makes a good point. I'm not getting anything done sitting here and no one is going to hand me anything. *Get up and get to work, Jenna!*

The cabin is made of logs, and so I think I can use the wood in the old woodpile that is too rotted to burn to build a wall down the middle of the cabin to enclose the part that is still in good shape. I might as well start on this before I mess with the woodstove because it is going to take me a long time to get this done, I'm afraid. I start the first of many trips in and out, choosing some of the logs in the best shape to put on the bottom with their ends facing my new room. I snug a second layer on top of them, and a third before I am too tired to continue. My new wall is up to my calf and the different colors of logs and all the growth rings look sort of pretty, if I say so myself. My work is interrupted by the discovery of a family of mice that are nesting in the pile. I put the log back and leave them undisturbed—there were three pink babies wriggling around—and they were super cute. All kinds of critters like to live in an old woodpile. I found a snakeskin and a very live salamander, shiny black with spots. He goggled his eyes at me and made his way off into the ferns with a rubbery wriggle. The few white grubs I uncovered went into my bait can. They are likely to catch some perch later.

I do a little math in my head and figure I have enough wood to complete the wall all the way up. That will seal off the chimney side from the wind and rain, a great improvement in a short time! I pace it off, and it leaves me a space three paces wide and four paces long, just a little bigger than Henry's cabin, I figure. When cold weather comes, I will do my best to use the woodstove for cooking and heating and I think I can take my tent into the root cellar and sleep down there. Those canning jars didn't break after four winters, so I don't think I'll freeze down there, either. Now I've got all that figured out—ha—take that, stupid Skip!

I've had a refreshing swim and caught three perch for dinner. Now, to get that stove going. First, I have to study this black metal box on legs. It is not too big, but I'm sure it will throw out a lot of heat, so this first fire should be small, as an experiment. The door squeaks as I open it and peer inside—a little rusty, I guess. As I clean out the ashes, I run into a couple of bird skeletons. Poor things must have gotten down the chimney and couldn't figure out how to get out. I get the stove all shoveled out and the ashes dumped outside in the woods. I build a small fire just the way I would do a campfire, and it seems to be going just great—a little smoky until I see a silver handle under the door and swing it to the right. That makes the smoke go up the chimney much better.

I go outside to retrieve my iron skillet by the campfire, but when go back in, dark smoke is belching out of the stove and the air is thick. What do I do? OMG, I am going to burn down the cabin—MY cabin! My dreams are beginning to go up in smoke, too. I run, choking, off the porch and down the front steps with a black cloud following me. Quick! I need to run back in there with water! My eyes are burning so much. I pull up my tee shirt to wipe the tears. Just then, a dark shape lumbers past me toward the cabin porch, spinning me around in my tracks. What's going on here? A deep voice commands me to go down by the pond and to stay there. It's Skip. He is in MY cabin shouting orders at ME! I hear banging and the sound of water sloshing around. Then, there is a long silence. Too long. Is he all right?

"Hey, are you okay? Are you okay?" Smoke is still pouring out of the door, but finally Skip staggers onto the porch and struggles down the steps. He has a red bandana held to his mouth and nose. His forehead is smudged with black smoke and it is obvious he cannot see through his coated glasses. His tee shirt and jeans are streaked with black, and a cloud of smoke follows him out of the cabin.

"Hell's, bells, kid! Whaddaya tryin' to do, start a forest fire?" He limps over and gets right in my face. "I got that fire of yours out, but somethin' is blockin' your chimney, and you coulda started a chimney fire, destroyed your cabin and everything for miles. I oughta turn you over my knee!"

"You try it and I'll kill you if you do." I pull out my knife and stand posed to run.

He looks sadly at me and then sits with a groan on a fallen log. He looks as exhausted as I am scared. My heart dances in my chest at the danger, the smoke, the fire, the human contact. The exertion of putting out the fire and the conflict with me is too much for him, and he doesn't even seem to be able to lift his arms. He draws in ragged breaths and coughs deeply and painfully. A profound hurt is in his eyes.

"Jenna." He says quietly.

"How do you know my name, you weirdo? You ARE stalking me. I knew it." I back up to the edge of the pond, ready to make a dash to my car. I can lock myself in, see if it starts, and get out of here.

He continued, quietly, patiently. "I told you a couple of weeks ago that I know your name because I knew your grandpa. Your Uncle Bill was my best friend in the world. You may not believe me, but I'm tellin' you the truth. I am not goin' to hurt you, but I have to stop playin' these childish games with you as if you are some sort of wild animal. I have to talk to you person to person, and you will listen to me." His tone commands me. "Sit down!"

I sit on a fallen log. I lay down the knife.

Skip pulls a clean handkerchief out of his pants pocket, breathes on his glasses, and cleans off the soot. He doesn't bother with his face. This situation has me on edge, but I figure I have to at least be civil to him because he holds my future in his hands now. He can go today and turn me into the authorities, and I will have to flee on foot or in the Buick, which hasn't been started in a month. He could have laughed and walked on by when he saw the smoke, but he didn't. He says he knew Uncle Bill, and maybe he did. That doesn't make him a good guy, but it makes me a little less afraid of him. So, I guess I owe it to him to sit here and listen to what he has to say for a few minutes.

"I haven't been stalkin' you in the way you think, but I walk by here to a good fishin' lake and to town a couple of times a week, and I have seen what you have accomplished. I thought you were just a runaway, at first. We get that here sometimes. I don't generally report them because in a day or so runaways move on, but when I saw you workin' to clean out the cabin, I knew you had a connection of some sort—and I finally figured it out. Bill wrote to me when I was in the Marines, said his sister and her little kid Jenna were spending some time with him away from the city. That would make you what, 14?"

"Fifteen." I reply quietly, my eyes on my dirty hands in my lap.

"You look skinny…been eatin' good?"

"I do alright for myself."

"I'm sure you do."

He has another coughing fit. We sit in silence for a while and when he finally catches his breath, he speaks again. He is no longer angry and now that he isn't being threatened at the point of a knife, we both relax a bit. "The smoke's cleared. Tell you what. Let's take a look at that chimney, eh?"

"Really?"

"Yup."

Skip showed me how he could scale a couple of the ends of the cabin logs and swing himself onto the roof over by the chimney—good leg first, and stiff one after. He peered into the chimney.

"There's a raccoon nest in there. No wonder she wouldn't draw. Grab me somethin' to break this up, eh."

I handed him a straight limb from over by the woodpile. "Will this do it?"

"Perfect. Now, step back."

He rammed the limb into the chimney, fishing out nesting debris, until the limb rattled free and ran up and down the chimney smoothly. A thick pillar of smoke rose. He pitched down the limb.

"Do you have to get up there and do that lots of times?"

"Naw—this is because no one's been here. Could use a critter screen over it, but it's okay for this winter."

Climbing down is harder for him with his stiff leg. He looks like he is going to slip on the last step, and I automatically reach out to steady him. The human touch sends something like an electric shock up my arm—it has been so long. I jerk my hand away. He doesn't comment.

"Before I leave I want to be sure you can handle this stove."

He leads me in and gives me a lesson about the kind of wood to burn, the levers that control the fire, and the safety thermometer that is built into the stovepipe. He teaches me all the special woodstove vocabulary, too, and makes me build a little fire then and there, like a final exam. This final exam means survival—not just a grade.

After our lesson, he looks around at my living space: the downed pine, the swept floors, the two chairs, the open root cellar trap door. His eyes light on my new building project.

"Is this firewood wall your idea?"

"Uh huh."

"It's really a great idea, Jenna. Got enough wood to finish it?"

"Yep."

"Well, you're set now, we are on speakin' terms, and I'm headin' out. I'm going to town tomorrow to get my mail and a few groceries. Can I pick up anythin' for you? How about some cornmeal to fry some corncakes to go with all that fish you've been catchin'. I know you have had good luck because it smells wonderful when I pass by your fire. Good for you, Jenna. Your Uncle Bill would be pleased."

I'm not sure about all of this, but hearing him say that gives me a warm feeling, and I find myself smiling at him for the first time. I am really getting low on beans and rice, my main calories. If I take him up on his offer, I wouldn't have to show up in town and explain myself, but I just can't quite let down my guard.

"Naw, I don't think so. Thanks, anyways."

"Well, okay. So long."

"So long."

As he turns to walk away, I quietly say, "Thanks, Skip, for helping me out."

"It's nothin'—what neighbors do."

Geez! Who does he think he is, Mr. Rogers? Neighbors in the middle of the woods? Good grief.

As I watch him go, I find myself checking out his limp and am glad it isn't worse after his adventure with the fire and on the roof. Why do I feel responsible for this guy who is nothing to me? Uncle Bill, why should I trust this man? I don't need a neighbor. I came here to disappear.

I suddenly hear Uncle Bill: *Jenna, the reason you were able to drive all the way up here in June was because nobody cared. They didn't care if you were a runaway, hurt, hungry, sick, broke, had a driver's license, underage, in serious trouble. They didn't care about your safety—only their paycheck. For some reason, you care. You have always cared. Who in the world taught you to care?*

"You did, Uncle Bill. You did." I say aloud to the setting sun.

Chapter 14

The next morning I continue work on my interior wall. I stand on a chair to climb onto the tree trunk to put the final layers in place and then stuff the gaps with shredded bark. It looks as if it will be effective at keeping out the cold. Yay, me! Climbing down, I pull two chairs close to the stove. The chapter I was reading in *Walden* must be in the back of my head. Time for a break. My copy is on the porch, so I find my bookmark and re-read the passage about chairs from last night:

I had three chairs in my house; one for solitude, two for friendship, three for society. One inconvenience I sometimes experienced in so small a house, the difficulty of getting to a sufficient distance from my guest when we began to utter the big thoughts in big words. You want room for your thoughts to get into sailing trim and run a course or two before they make their port. The bullet of your thought must have overcome its lateral and ricochet motion and fallen into its last and steady course before it reaches the ear of the hearer, else it may plough out again through the side of his head. That makes me laugh thinking about ideas flying around in the air like bullets, but I can see some truth in maybe having to slow down your thoughts to allow another person to be able to grab them with their brain. It's a funny image I will draw in my sketchbook. Anyways, two chairs are plenty for my house—and it's too early to think about having a friend.

It has been five days since I have heard the *swish, thump* of Skip's walk past the lake. Maybe I've been too busy with my wall project and gathering wood to hear him come and go, but I'm sort of worried. Heck, it's weird I was so scared of him and now I'm worried that something is wrong with him. That's nuts! Something must be wrong with me! Must be ESP 'cause, speak of the devil, here he comes now through the ferns.

"Halloo in the house!"

"Hi."

"Got a few things in town today for ya."

"You didn't have to do that."

"Know it, but I figured you could use some cornmeal, Crisco, and small bags of flour, rice, and beans, a bar of castile soap, pound of bacon. Even bought some sugar. I kept half the sugar and brought the rest over. Better for you if you keep away from that stuff, but I still like it in my coffee. Habit, I guess. Where do you want me to put this stuff?"

He barged past me and set everything down by the trapdoor. "Got your wall done, I see. Looks good. Here's the bill. He stuck it on a nail in the wall by the woodstove. Pay me all or part of it when you can. The bacon and sugar is on me. Gotta get home. See you later!"

I don't want to go out to the car and give away the hiding place of my few precious dollars, so I mumble my thanks and promise I'll make good on it next time I see him. He nods, turns around and walks away with his halting gait. In the back of my brain I was hoping he'd stick around for a few minutes, try out my second chair, but I don't want to beg him to stay, so I can only stand and watch him lurch off into the trees. I store my groceries and get ready to cook a good dinner. Guess that's just the way it is going to be with my neighbor.

Soon the fragrance of sweet hickory bacon fills the cabin. Oh, my!! I use the grease to fry up some cornmeal cakes that taste like heaven.

I'm adding to my woodpile for winter, filling the pages of my sketchpad with charcoal and pen and ink drawings, and working my way through Henry's book. Lots of *Walden* seems impossible for me to understand, and whole pages of it are old school and boring, but every once in a while there is something that hits home when I stop and think about it. He wrote: *what old people say you cannot do you try and find that you can. Old deeds for old people, and new deeds for new. Confucius says to know that we know what we know, and that we do not know what we do not know, that is true knowledge.* That little puzzle stopped me in my tracks, but it makes sense after you untangle the words. My time in the woods has taught me that I gain a tiny bit more knowledge every day, but there are many more things I do not know, and I'm not too proud to admit it. I wish I knew more about the living things around me and could capture images in my artwork lots better. Henry tells me to just keep living each day, spending time really seeing with my eyes and learning from nature. This place is my school, and all the living things around me are trying to teach me to live, too. *Keep your eyes, ears, and heart open, Jenna!*

Chapter 15

I have a little fire going in the stove. I am warming a dishpan of water—another score from the root cellar—to wash my face and hands after a day of gathering wood in the mist. I'm chilled to the bone, dog-tired, and hungry.

Skip materializes out of the fog. He is wearing a backpack with a flapping poncho over it all and is carrying a thermos bottle. Looks like maybe he wants to have a visit, and I'm hoping he has something good to eat in that backpack. I'm still dreaming about that crispy bacon that is long gone.

"Hello in the house," he shouts.

"Hi. Do you want to come in for a minute out of the rain?"

"Sure. Brought you somethin'."

"You don't need to keep doing that, you know."

"Here's a thermos of coffee—don't know if you have the habit—but thought maybe you wanna start. Next to beer, it's the UP's most popular beverage. Got a couple of cups? I tried my hand at some molasses cookies—Mother's recipe."

The cookies emerge from a paper bag mostly crushed. "Ope."

"That's okay. They look good, but I'll bet your mother never burned them," I tease him with a grin.

"Beggars can't be choosers, Missy."

We settle onto the two chairs by the stove. The coffee is hot, dark and sweet, not too bad, and the cup warms my palms.

He pulls out his smoking pipe and fills it with tobacco from a leather pouch. "Hope you don't mind."

"Nah."

A wisp of fragrant smoke soon curls from the bowl and he sits back with a sigh. He stretches his legs out in front of him and looks over at me with a little smile.

"How's it goin' for ya, kid? Really. No bull."

"I'm doing fine. The stuff you bought me from the store helped. I've got the money in my pocket to pay you. Been carrying it around until next time I saw you." I dig $23 out of my pocket and count it out. He pulls the receipt off the nail and tosses it into the woodstove. "OK. We're square."

The woodstove crackles and we sit in silence for a while, eating the cookies—not too bad if you break off the blackened edges—and sipping a second cup of coffee.

Something is up with him—gnawing at him. He's not interested in small talk, that's for sure. I sit quietly and just wait, watching the wisps of smoke curl drift around his head. He isn't looking at me, just staring out the window at the misty pines and the red squirrels scampering on my growing woodpile.

When he finally speaks, his voice is deep and quiet, almost a whisper. "She loved me, dontcha know."

This is totally out of the blue. OMG, stuff's getting weird here. "What? Who?"

"Your mom."

Squirming in my chair, I can't find any words. I'm dreading the story I don't know if I want to hear about a woman and a life I'm trying to put behind me. I feel my heartbeat rise and catch my breath. My first thought is to stand, push this man out the door, and lock it behind him, but I'm unable to move a muscle. I will my ears not to hear, fearful of what he is going to say. He still is looking out the window—lost in memories.

"Yup," he goes on calmly, "Your mom and I went together for two years in high school. I had plans for us. Day we graduated in the spring of 2000, I asked Alissa to marry me.

G*eez. Stop right now, please*, I silently beg, but he forges ahead.

"Bill had a job lined up for me workin' timber with him. Dad offered me a piece of land for a cabin. I had it all worked out: good payin' job, place to call our own built just the way she wanted it. I was pretty excited to go down on one knee and show Alissa the little chip of a diamond I had bought her. He pauses and takes a deep breath and a sigh, "She turned me down.

"She said she loved me, but she didn't want to be a Yooper stuck up here in the boondocks, livin' with her dad and brother in the little frame house in Birch Bay where she had grown up. She didn't want to live out in the woods with me, either. She was dreamin' of life in the city—the big city, not just Marquette or Houghton—goin' to college—meetin' new people—makin' it big in the real world. She knew I couldn't leave the woods and lakes.

"I kept after her for a month, followed her around like a lost puppy. I even worked up the nerve to offer to go along just to keep her in my life. I guess she got sick of me and her folks badgerin' her because she packed her a bag and musta caught a bus or somethin', because she was just gone. Just gone." Skip sighs again deeply.

"That was it. She left a letter for her folks, but didn't write after that. I drove my beater downstate thinkin' maybe I could find her—shows what a stupid kid I was—but desperate because my heart was broken and I couldn't eat or sleep. Wishful thinkin' gets you nowhere in this life."

He falls silent then, drifting in the past, but, no matter how painful, I suddenly need to know more. This has all of a sudden become the story of MY life, too, with blank spaces that need filling if I am ever to feel right.

"What did you do then?" I quietly ask.

"I came home with my tail draggin'. Nothin' seemed to matter to me. Next day, I drove into Marquette and signed up with the Marines. I was so low and beat up, I didn't feel much like a man. Always heard the Marines made mice into men, and I was a daggone mouse.

"I got through trainin' at Parris Island okay, and the first four years I was assigned to basic guard duty stateside. It was borin', but kept my mind off home, and I was puttin' aside a little money. In 2004, I signed up for another stint because the US had invaded Iraq and I was hopin' to get into the action over there. I later figured out the conflict was mostly about oil, but also the US was personally mad at a man named Saddam Hussein, but I found myself, shaved head, disciplined, and well trained, over there with my band of brothers clearin' out little villages, hatin' people and aimin' my gun at everyone. When I wasn't shootin' at the enemy, my adrenaline was firin' like crazy—a real man, for sure. I got my wish to see plenty of action—more than I had bargained for.

"I spent three years in that dusty, dry country. Then an IED took off my left foot while we were movin' down a path from one village to another, and a piece of shrapnel took out my right eye." He pulls up his left pant leg and there it is—all metal and pink plastic above his drooping, striped sock—gross. He sees me grimace.

"Yup. Left foot and right brown eye compliments of the VA. Spent two years at Walter Reed Hospital recoverin' from my nasty head injury, gettin' fitted with these replacement parts and doin' rehab. I was in bad shape and an ornery patient. That's when Bill found out I was back stateside in the hospital. He called and told me you and Alissa was at the cabin with him for a month. He let me know your father had died in a car accident, and your mom seemed to be strugglin'. She needed Bill's help sortin' out her finances and figurin' out how to use the life insurance policy to support the two of you. She was sad and lonely. He said he would do his best to try to convince her to come back north and raise you here—he would try his darndest to get you both to wait for me—but my docs wouldn't let me go anywhere. I asked Bill to have your mom call me, but she never did. Later that summer I called again. Bill said you both had gone back to Chicago. Your mom had landed a new job at a bakery, and the life insurance was still helpin' to pay the mortgage for your house somewhere in the suburbs. She wouldn't listen about stayin' up north.

"Didn't seem to be much reason to hurry home to nothin', so I spent three more years in Maryland workin' as a janitor at the military hospital, livin' with some other vets, sowin' some wild oats and gettin' in trouble with alcohol and bar fights. Kinda lost track of time. Guess I still had something to prove about bein' a man. The downtown cops got to know me by name after haulin' me to the drunk tank lotsa times. They had a nickname for me—called me The Gimp.

"I'd lost my mom way back as a teenager, and Dad passed away durin' my stateside stint with the Marines. I inherited his land and rundown house but sold most of it right away—keepin' 80 acres of woods. I woke up one morning, hungover and miserable, and decided I had to come back to the UP—the only place that held some good memories of the past. I figured my current situation was pitiful and my future was pretty much shot. I was lookin' to get away from the world and hide. Keep people from pityin' me for my fake eye and my limp. The women I met out East always treated me like I was the ugly puppy in the pound—fun to talk sweet to and laugh with for one evenin', but never to take home.

Bill met me at the bus station and drove me to my woods. He had set up camp for me with a tent, food cache, and basic hand tools. I picked up an axe and started to fell trees. A couple of months of hard, painful work sweated all the alcohol and most of the daily anger and bad dreams out of my system. Log by log, I singlehandedly fashioned the little cabin I had dreamed about livin' in with your mom. I've had five years to rattle around in it as a bachelor. It's a house, but not a home.

"Bill told me that first summer you were a little tyke, you loved to watch bugs and carry frogs in the front pocket of your overalls. That you sat on the bank and watched him fish, and they had to watch you every minute from jumpin' into the pond to catch minnows. Your face lighted up at the sight of dragonflies and you ran all over tweetin' and singin'—claimed you were talkin' to the birds.

"He loved you with all his heart. Havin' you here brightened up his bachelor life. When we talked on the phone, he would tell me how he looked forward to drivin' down to Wisconsin, meetin' your mom halfway for a visit and meal at the Village Inn, and then bringin' you up north. You probably never knew but he sent money, too, when he could, to help you stay in your house down there. Alissa was his only sister, and he loved her, too." He pauses, coughs deeply, and sits forward.

"Well, that's about it." He pushes off from the chair and stands up suddenly. He can't look at me. He's embarrassed about sharing all these pent up emotions and obviously can't wait to leave.

Well, that may have been it for him, but it sure is more than I have bargained for: totally TMI. I have listened to this tumble of words with a stony silence, barely breathing. I can't look at him, either, and study the floor.

He sighs and speaks up loudly now with urgency, "This is ancient history and it probably don't matter to you. I've talked way too much—more than I've said in one stretch for years. Looks like the rain's pickin' up. I'll be movin' along now." And, like that, he sweeps his stuff together and is out the door, quickly disappearing into the mist and ferns. *Swish, thump, swish, thump.*

Something comes over me. I don't want to do this, but my body and heart betray my mind, and I am somehow swept out into the rain behind him. "Skip—come back here—please."

The mist plays around us as I pour out my mother's story—and my story—details I have never revealed to anyone. I cry and shiver from shock and grief. He hands me a grubby handkerchief from his coat pocket and guides me by the shoulders inside and back to my chair by the fire, tosses in a couple more sticks, puts a flannel shirt around my shoulders, and pours me the last few drops of coffee. Chair legs scrape the floor as he pulls his chair over to face mine. He sits, elbows on knees, head hanging, and waits for me to calm down. Our knees are touching. As I finally raise my head, I see sorrow and concern for me deeply etched into his brow.

"Jenna, I had no idea."

"I know. Mom and I were totally alone."

"I wish she had figured out how to get ahold of me."

"She was too sick, Skip. Everything was hopeless and painkillers ruled her heart, body, and soul in the last three or four years. When she got to that point, I didn't even matter to her. I feel guilty because I was so angry at her and only wanted to run so fast and as far as I could when she died. She didn't seem like my mom any more, but I just left her there, Skip. Like she was nothing to me. All alone." I thought I was all out of tears, but they spring to my eyes—and to his, as well. We sit in silence for a long time again. Then he gives a great shuddering sigh, hands slap his thighs, and he sits up straight with a new energy.

"Well, this explains a lot of stuff, but we can't go backwards, kid. Gotta figure out how to move on, and you are makin' a good start of it. I keep thinkin', I coulda, shoulda, woulda been your dad."

"Aw, don't go there."

"Can't help it. Been thinkin' a lot about your mom and Bill since you showed up. Thought I had a handle on these memories. That was part of the drinkin' to forget, I guess, but maybe it's okay for you and me to do some rememberin' together."

"Skip, I have been dreading this question, but Mom never told me. How did Uncle Bill die?"

"You don't know?"

"No. Will you tell me, please? I don't really want to think about it, but I need to know."

"Okay, Jenna." He pauses to put his thoughts in order. "At the end of September four years ago, I was puttin' the finishin' touches on my cabin, and he stopped by to ask me to go duck huntin' the next day. I was to meet him at his blind at dawn. When I arrived quietly in the early mornin' light, he looked to be sound asleep in the blind, coat and hat on, his shotgun across his lap—so peaceful it made me smile because he looked like he was havin' the best dream ever. I whispered to him so's not to scare any ducks, and got no response—shook him a little to wake him up and then realized he was gone, just like that. I had seen enough death in war to know there was no reason to run for help, so he and I sat there for a couple of hours. I talked and he listened. I poured it all out like I've done today. Mostly told him how p.o.ed I was that he left me just when we had plans to live our lives out as huntin' and fishin' buddies. I've felt all alone for four years, too, kid." He swipes at the tears on his cheeks. I busy myself with stirring the fire and pretend not to see his distress.

"Skip, you are gonna think I'm crazy, but Uncle Bill is in my dreams, and I have actually felt and heard him in the room with me. Mom, too, from back when she was well."

He smiled a wistful smile, "That's not crazy, Jenna. Us loners feel other people around us all the time. We have the time and the quiet for the memories, if we aren't afraid to let them come, eh."

"Guess that's it."

"Are you gonna be okay if I head home?"

"Yep. Got a lot to think about. You?"

"Yeah, me too. She called me Skippy, dontcha know?"

"Mom did?"

"Yeah. She said it was because I was chunky." It's a relief to find something to lighten the mood, and we both chuckle at that. I'm totally exhausted, and I can tell he is, too.

He rises and heads out the door. I call to his back, "Skippy, I think you are smooth."

His laugh echoes over the pond into the pines. "That's what I used to tell Alissa all the time."

A ray of sunlight filters down onto the water and sends a shimmer to light his path home.

Chapter 16

This is a delicious evening, when the whole body is one sense, and imbibes delight through every pore. I go and come with a strange liberty in Nature, a part of herself. As I walk along the stony shore of the pond in my shirt sleeves, though it is cool as well as cloudy and windy.... The bullfrogs trump to usher in the night, and the note of the whippoorwill is borne on the rippling wind from over the water. Sympathy with the fluttering alder and poplar leaves almost takes away my breath; yet, like the lake, my serenity is rippled but not ruffled. I lift my eyes from *Walden* and look over at my latest sketch of my rippling pond. Water is so hard to capture on paper, but I'm making progress. I always thought that water was blue, but now I can see a confusing range of colors that swirl and blend and shimmer. How do you possibly draw or paint a shimmer? My notebook is full on one side and I'm starting to draw on the backs of the pages.

I cut my 69th notch this morning before coming out to draw. I'm filling hot summer days with harvesting and drying fruit, reading, drawing, and sleeping deep uninterrupted hours. Skip is a constant in my life—not bugging me but checking in regularly. I admit it feels good to know someone has my back and is to be trusted. He's been bringing me supplies from the store once in a while. I'm down to my last $50, but I want to keep that much cash just in case something unexpected comes up, so I'm still hiding it.

Thimbleberries are all over the place. Sweet and beautiful, they remind me of the red raspberries I used to see at the grocery but that Mom and I could never afford: little ruby jewels. I have picked all I can find, and Skip showed me how to put them out on the porch on an old window screen to dry them like the Chippewa used to do back in the day. There are also small apples and pears forming on a couple of old orchard trees near the cabin. Those won't be ready to pick for a while, yet. I've poured over the two copies of *Mother Earth News* Skip brought over. The one has a recipe for making apple leather. Fruit rollups came with our school lunches once in a while. I really liked those, and bet I can make them even better on my trusty old woodstove.

Henry has a funny part in his book where he writes: *One farmer said to me, "you cannot live on vegetable food solely, for it furnishes nothing to make bones with,"… walking all the while he talks behind his oxen, which, with vegetable-made bones, jerk him and his lumbering plough along in spite of every obstacle.*" Ha. I'm getting along pretty well with beans and rice, fruit, and a fish fry once in a while. I have new muscles and I'm tan—feeling really good. My heart is lighter now I'm not holding in secrets. One person knows what I am all about, and he is a rock. The days are flying by in my little cabin by the water.

Chapter 17

"Hello in the house! Dang, girl! This place is lookin' like a beaver palace." Skip has skirted my huge woodpile of sticks and caught me making my 134th mark on the doorframe. The little whittlings begin at elbow level on the frame and head upwards in groups of seven and are running along the top of the door. I have to stand on a chair to do a nice job of them. I'm proud of over 19 weeks of independent living on my pond. These marks are a daily reminder of my worth and accomplishments, and Skip knows it. He runs his hands over the doorframe and smiles up at me.

"These are like the notches my dad used to make inside the broom closet door to record how fast us kids were growin'. It's neat, Jenna. Got any coffee?"

While I put on the coffee pot, Skip picks up my drawing pad and looks at my newest pen and ink drawings shaded with charcoal. I've been spending time drawing outdoors and from memory in the evenings now that the days are getting shorter. I'm pretty pleased with my progress on capturing landscapes: the pond, the waterfall where I fill my water jugs, the pines and birches. Sometimes, I like to add some of Henry's wisdom on the pages, too.

Skip plunks down in his favorite chair, lights up his pipe, leans back, and delivers a dose of reality. "It's October 15. Sorry it's been so long since I stopped by, but I've been putting up wood at my place, too. We will be havin' our first hard frost and maybe snow very soon. You ready? Winter's a six month affair up here."

"I dunno."

"Lookin' around, I'd say you are in pretty good shape. What's the survival plan?"

I explain how I am going to move my bed down into the root cellar after the first really frosty night, and he thinks that is a good idea. He climbs awkwardly down the cellar ladder after me, and I show him my apple leather and dried thimbleberries to provide vitamins and calories this winter. He inspects the contents of Bill's clothing trunk and I can see the wheels turning.

"I can't wear my old pac boots with his foot of mine—had to get 'em custom-made—so you can have my old ones. They won't be much too big with these thick socks. I'll teach you to make a fur hat and a pair of leather choppers."

We climb back up into the warmth of the stove. "You'll be all right. You're not getting' too lonely, are you?"

"Nah."

"Well, guess you've got old Henry to keep you company." He nods toward my copy of *Walden.* "Makin' heads or tails of it? Your Uncle Bill was nuts about that guy. I'm more of a fan of Mark Twain, myself. He wrote: *'It's not the size of the dog in the fight, it's the size of the fight in the dog.'"*

I smile. "Guess that's sort of like me, right?"

"Yup," he chuckles. "I'm headed to town. Need anythin'?"

"Nah."

"Okay. "

"Hey, Skip—would it be easier for you to drive my car into town? It's just sitting here useless. The battery may be dead as a doornail, though."

Skip laughs at my old-fashioned saying. "Well, it's a good idea, but no thanks. If I did that, there would be lots of questions about that vehicle, and you and me don't need that. Also, I need to walk. Use it or lose it, dontcha know? Wouldn't hurt to start that thing once in a while, though. Next time I'm by, we'll try to crank her over."

"OK."

"By the way, I think you've got plenty of wood there. Get out and enjoy this last little bit of warmth while you can, eh."

I get back up on my chair and turn back to cutting the perfect notch for today. I'm grateful for each of these days, and I run my fingers over all the notches, one by one.

Chapter 18

I sit back with a cup of coffee in hand and take a minute to look around me with satisfaction. Outside, our first snow is coming down right on schedule, wet and heavy, but I am snug in my cabin. My woodpile is quickly disappearing under a creamy white covering. The little red squirrels seem to be delighted by the early snow and are zipping here and there all around the side yard and up and over the outhouse. Using the facility is a challenge these days with the frigid toilet seat and the cold wind off the lake, but I have to deal with what I've got. I'm content with using water in my dishpan for washing up this winter. I have been pulling my hair back and putting it in one long braid that is reaching down to the middle of my shoulder blades. I don't need to wash my hair very often, and the dishpan works for that, too. I'm not getting dirty these days—not like in the heat of the summer when I was working like crazy to get ready for lazy days like this.

My root cellar is working great for sleeping. I feel so secure down there, surrounded by all my food and possessions. I'm glad Uncle Bill dug it so big because the shelves are full right now. I got rid of all the old home canned goods, scrubbed the jars with sand and lake water and dried them well. I have jars of dried berries: thimbleberries, raspberries, wild blueberries. Other jars hold dried apples, dried pears, fruit leather, and dried mushrooms that were approved by Skip as safe to eat. One was a white puffball as big as my head! Skip made several more trips to the store and spent every dime I had on a big bag of oatmeal, dried milk, toilet paper, beef jerky, matches, and he found a sale on veggies: green beans and corn. The corned beef hash he bought me—because it is his favorite—smelled kind of gross in the can, but tasted really yummy when I fried it up: salty and peppery. Along with big bags of dried beans, rice, and cornmeal, I'm in pretty good shape. He even brings me a dozen eggs from his chickens once in a while.

I've run up a pretty thick pile of store receipts on the nail, but Skip tells me I will be able to get squared up with him after I help him when he goes deer hunting next month. He says we will be making venison jerky and he will share some. Wonder if I will like it. Well, as Skip says, beggars can't be choosers. Food has just become fuel to keep me going. It doesn't have to be delicious or anything, but once in a while I crave a burger and a greasy bag of salty fries.

I look down at my jeans—poor things—there is a rip in one knee and my ankles are hanging out. The new muscles in my thighs and calves are defined by the denim. I feel sort of like Hulk busting out of my clothes. Guess it is time to raid Uncle Bill's chest and dig out some long underwear and wool pants.

We used to tease him about wearing faded, baggy, red long johns. He kept them on under his clothes until the pond was warm enough to take a swim, sometimes all the way to July. Then, like flipping a switch, he would take down his winter clothes from the pegs on the wall in his room, pack them away in the trunk, and get out his three Hawaiian shirts and two pairs of khaki shorts. That worked until the pond got too cold, and then out came the long johns again. I can hear him loudly state, "Don't make fun of my union suit. Greatest invention ever was." He liked to gross us out with the story of the old timer who kept his union suit on full-time for several years, wearing it even into the few showers he took. When he had to go into the hospital for tests, they had to actually cut off the suit because his leg and arm hairs had grown right through! EWWWW! I think he made that up, but the thought of it gave us all the willies and made us laugh.

Sure enough, the familiar, bright red union suit is in the chest. I pull it on just for fun. Wow! It really is warm and covers me neck to wrists to ankles. Pulling the rear of them around, I discover the drop seat fastened with two buttons. Good grief! But, I leave them on and add a pair of wool pants that aren't too bad a fit. I really have grown in the last few months. There are big, wooly socks, a bulky fisherman's sweater, several turtleneck pullovers, and a down jacket patched here and there with silver duct tape to keep the feathers from leaking out. I carry the pile of clothes up the ladder and put on all the layers in front of the warm stove. Skip has brought over his pack boots, so I slip them on and make my way for a visit to the outhouse. That is where I discover the marvelous invention of the drop seat. No need to strip down to your underwear to use the toilet like we little girls used to have to do when we had on snowsuits. Just lower pants, unbutton the union suit seat, get the flap out of the way, sit down on the cold seat, and go potty wrapped in relative warmth while contemplating the slush growing on the surface of the pond. *I'm not making fun now, Uncle Bill!*

Chapter 19

I set out on a sunny day to fill my water jugs, boots making a fresh path in six inches of new snow. The woods sparkles around me as I walk several miles to the place where the water runs the freshest. I can see where a fox has cruised across the trail. He has made tracks in the snow in a straight line like stitches on a quilt, and there are doe prints, too. Snow has settled in great mounds on the evergreen boughs, weighing many of them all the way to the ground. The air is crisp and clean with a gentle snow sifting down from the trees—sorta like being in a snow globe. Yesterday, I stayed in all day watching it snow and doing some more sketching wrapped cozy in the fisherman sweater.

A big pileated woodpecker is hammering on a dead tree. *Bam, bam, bam, bam.* How does his little brain stand the abuse, as big chips of bark and decayed wood rain down onto the snow? Skip explained some people think woodpeckers have extra space and padding in their skulls to cushion their brains, but other ornithologists think their birdbrains can take a beating and still work. Birds are really amazing creatures. The gorgeous black and white bird with the bright red crest sees me coming and pushes off from the tree with a loud complaint. He swoops through the pines letting everyone in the woods know I'm coming. *Chee chee chee chee chee be bop! Chee chee chee chee chee be bop!!*

As I approach the stream with my gallon jugs, something just doesn't seem right. I stop dead in my tracks. Fresh boot prints in the snow. Skip must have passed by here on his trap line. But, wait a minute, there are several places where the prints are crystal clear. I stop and study them. The fresh impressions are made by a small hiking boot with deep tread—much smaller than my shoe size. A walking stick or ski pole is poked into the snow at intervals, too. The tracks have come from over the ridge to the south, zig zag down to the stream, pass by my watering spot at the waterfall, and then wind off to the west, disappearing into the woods.

This is spooky, and I take several steps into the deeper snow on the side of the trail to crouch behind a spruce tree. I slowly look all around me, scanning the forest for the sight of a stranger, perhaps a bit of color out of place in the whiteness, but nothing is to be seen. My breath sends out white vapor clouds that hover before my eyes. After several minutes of deep silence, I walk cautiously back to the stream. As I kneel down to fill my water jug, I keep my eyes trained around me. I want to get this job done and get out of here. These footprints were made today, but if I get my jugs filled and head home, the falling snow will quickly cover up my own tracks and, hopefully, not lead anyone to my cabin.

My eyes must be playing tricks on me! A bright red envelope is hanging on an evergreen bough like a Christmas ornament. It's placed where I can't miss seeing it. It can't be meant for me; it must be for

Skip. He's the only other resident of this neck of the woods. I'll take it to him. I snatch it off the tree and stuff it in my pocket as I flee down my trail toward home.

I arrive at the cabin out of breath and sweaty under my heavy coat. I'm jumpy and feeling paranoid for the first time in several months. I realize, too late, I should have taken a long, confusing route home to discourage anyone from following. *Please, don't let this screw things up!*

The envelope is not sealed, and my curiosity gets the better of me. Inside is a short note written on thick paper in, what has to be, a delicate woman's hand.

You have nothing to fear from me. I often visit this waterfall on my hikes and twice I have seen you here getting water. I will not try to find you, but I want you to know I am here for you, as a friend. I care about your safety. If you wish to contact me, leave a message behind the giant beech tree at the waterfall. It is unsigned.

I read the note twice. Dang! Someone has been spying on me. I don't know why it makes me so angry, but I feel violated. Another person has all of a sudden gained a powerful advantage over me, and there isn't anything I can do about it except play along with some sort of stupid game of hide and seek. Need help? Leave messages behind a frickin' tree? For Pete's sake! Why can't this female just keep her nose out of my business?

Chapter 20

I marked my 170th day today. Whoever left that note has been good for her word, so far. I'm not going back any time soon to get more water. Melting snow is working out well for me, and the flavor is nice for a change. I don't have to use purifying tablets in it, but it takes a ton of snow to melt down to make coffee or to cook my rice and beans. I never realized that a big dishpan of snow only melts into a cup or two of water. Water is precious.

I have to put thoughts of that meddling female behind me to help Skip with the deer hunt. I showed him the note, and he didn't have any idea who could have left it—must be someone from Birch Bay was his idea—and he assured me those people are pretty chill about letting others be. I'm trying to just forget about it.

"Hello in the house!"

"Hi…c'mon in."

"If you're goin' out with me to my deer blind, you need a few things. He handed me a brown paper shopping bag."

"What's that big smile for, Skip?"

"Aww, just open it, will ya?"

I reach into the bag and pull out a hat fashioned of fox skin—the lining hand stitched. Soft and light as a cloud.

"Stick it on, eh?"

It fits perfectly. The red, warm fur frames my face, and I tie the soft earflaps under my chin with the deerskin laces. I never had a gift like this before in my life, and tears begin to well in my eyes.

"Gosh, Skip."

"Wait, wait! There's more." In the bag is a pair of choppers—mittens designed for work with a thick but flexible deerskin outer layer lined with rabbit fur.

I put them on and do a little pirouette like a princess so he can see how wonderful his handcrafted gifts are and how happy they have made me. We both laugh at the fun of it. He blushes and looks at the floor like a shy teenage boy, and I feel like Cinderella at the ball!

Skip raises his head with a grin, "Before you go all fancy and girly girly on me, I need to tell you that those choppers are goin' to see some hard, dirty, bloody work and won't be so pretty after these next two weeks, but I'll come over this winter and teach you how to make a pair of your own. You can keep a clean pair for when you want to be glamorous and impress the porcupines and red squirrels, eh." We have a good laugh. I fix a pot of coffee and he fills me in on his hunting plan.

The next morning, dawn finds us dressed in hunter orange and hunkered down in Skip's makeshift deer blind made from long strips of bark leaning teepee style up against a big birch not too far from my cabin. Just enough cover to break up the human form, Skip explained. He has given me a lesson about how to load his rifle, prepare it to shoot, and put on the safety. He explains that since he has lost his right eye, he has had to learn to shoot left-eyed with the gun stock on his left shoulder. I still don't want to touch a gun, but I nod and watch politely.

We keep our voices to a whisper—or don't speak at all. I mostly curl up trying to stay warm.

Skip leans over and whispers, "I always get one in the first few hours of the openin' day because I do a lot of scoutin' and trackin' throughout the year and know where the deer yard up and travel to water. I'm not aimin' to take a big buck. Braggin' rights don't do anythin' for me, and I can't haul it in to the buck pole anymore to try to win a prize. What I'm lookin' for is a doe that has some fat on her and looks very healthy. This is a well-traveled deer trail. One will be along before too long and then the work begins." He settles back against the tree, his rifle across his lap.

I have fallen into a doze—hunting seems really boring—when I feel Skip's shoulder move as he raises his rifle, carefully takes aim, and pulls the trigger—one, two, three—quickly, smoothly, and just like that. The resounding explosion is deafening in the blind and scares the wits out of sleepy me for a moment. I jerk my elbows and head painfully back against the tree and my heart pounds with an adrenaline rush. I look over at Skip, who has turned to smile at me and my reaction to his shot.

"She's a nice doe, Jenna. Just what I was after. Clean shot to the heart and down she went before she ever knew what hit her. I just need to sit here for a moment and catch my breath. My heart is racing, too, kid."

I've been dreading watching Skip cut up a deer, but the process is actually very interesting, and he explains everything as he goes along. I help him shove the deer carcass onto its back. He uses a super sharp knife to make a cut all the way from between the back legs to the throat, exposing all the organs. He points out the heart, lungs, stomach, liver, intestines, and windpipe.

"Geez, Jenna. Back up a little and get out of my way, eh. You'd think this was biology class." He chuckles, nudges me out of the way good-naturedly, and goes to work making his important cuts. He gives the orders and I help him turn the deer this way and that, all the while Skip is carefully cutting the connecting tissue. With a couple of big yanks, all the innards are out on the ground in one piece. He works quickly and efficiently.

"You're a big help today, Jenna. Most people go into the grocery and don't know or care where the meat comes from or how the animal is handled. Just grab a foam tray wrapped in plastic wrap and go. Getting' venison from the woods is a lot more work, but it's satisfyin' to know this animal has lived a good, free life up to today and is taken with respect and thanks. I'm not a big meat-eater, so the venison I get from her will last me all year with a little to share with you, too."

"How do you keep all this meat good without electricity?"

"I can the best cuts with a pressure cooker on my cookstove, grind up some to make sausage to smoke in my smoke house, and dry the last of it into strips of jerky, flavored with garlic, salt, and pepper. Tonight, I'll have liver and onions! Want to join me?"

"Only tried it once—never again!"

I sit down and watch Skip work. There is no wasted movement as he uses several different shapes of knives and a little saw to finish what he tells me is called field dressing. Finally, he sends me to find a large plastic sled he had hidden in the trees. I help him pack the sled with the deer, which has become venison before my eyes. A living thing that, in a short time, has been transformed into protein to keep Skip fed throughout the year. It's like the fish that have been a great source of food for me. For some reason, I thought it was okay to kill a fish but not a deer. I am wrong about that. If it is wrong to eat venison, it is wrong to eat bacon or fish. I'm going to have to think about this for a while.

"What are you doing over there?" Skip had pulled the sled off to the side and looked like he was cleaning up the area.

"Come give me a hand, Jenna, and I'll tell you. As a kid, I used to hunt with a man from the Chippewa tribe. He taught me the way to pay the animal final respect. After givin' thanks for the successful kill and doin' field dressin', all that is left here on the ground will feed the coyotes and raptors. Red squirrels and porkies will gnaw on the bones, and the rest will go back to enrich the soil. Nothin' is wasted. Before we go, we need to take a moment to do somethin'."

He begins to lay the remains of the deer in a pattern in the bloody snow. I see what he is doing and join in. We arrange the leftover body parts as if the deer were lying here whole: head to the left, entrails laid out left to right, forelegs in running position. We step back and stand in silence for a moment. I don't know why, but there is something strangely beautiful to be found in this death.

"My friend told me this little ritual honors and thanks the deer for its sacrifice and allows it to run into the Hereafter. Can you feel it, too? Sure beats buyin' meat wrapped in plastic, don't it?" He assures me he can easily handle the sled to get home and, after a hug and thanks, we part ways.

As always, Skip's given me a lot to think about.

Chapter 21

182nd day today—26 weeks—exactly half a year at Loon Haven! The snow has been getting deeper and deeper. Skip has lent me some snowshoes so I can get around. It is a sunny December day, nearing Christmas; sunshine is so rare, I have to take advantage of it. I've got cabin fever, so I decide to take my drawing tablet out to make some winter sketches. Snow on the pine boughs is so wonderful because it makes all sorts of magical shapes like a fantasy world. I want to be able to capture the free-flowing lines with minimal crosshatching and subtle charcoal shading. I never realized how snow takes on such different tones of gray and picks up colors from the sky and trees and overlapping shadows. It's amazing!

I haven't been to the waterfall since that nosey female left that note, but my feet seem to automatically take me there as I muse and wander. It's still way below freezing, but the sun allows me to slip off my mitts and use my ink pen on my tablet. I have to warm the pen inside my coat once in a while to keep the ink flowing. I sit on a stump and try to capture the movement of the waterfall as the frigid water flows under the ice, bubbling and swirling. I have one of Henry's quotations in mind to use along with this drawing of the beautifully flowing water and reflected sky: *Heaven is under our feet as well as over our heads.*

Lost in my thoughts, I didn't notice them at first, but there they are again. Several days old, but distinct—the tracks of snowshoes smaller than mine. They come from over the ridge, through the deep snow, as before, to the watering spot, swing in an arc to the large beech tree, and head back up the ridge—a shorter hike today for this person who is invading my territory.

Just for curiosity's sake, I stand and advance to the big gray tree. Peeking around the huge trunk, I find a large transparent bin like they sell at Walmart for packing stuff up and storing it in a closet. What's up with this? I brush several inches of snow off the top. What the heck, might as well see what she has in mind. Lifting the lid, I find items it seems like I haven't seen for a lifetime…shampoo, conditioner, scissors, Gummy Bears, trail mix, toilet paper, toothpaste, toothbrush, and good smelling hand soap. OMG. There are two packages of old fashioned pads for my periods—aw, she's gone too far! That's so creepy, I can't believe it! I can't accept all this stuff, but it has to be intended for me.

I shut the box, walk back to the tree stump and sit down to think about all of this and the possible consequences of getting involved with this woman. The sun is warm on my furry hat, and I'm reminded of the joy Skip had in watching me accept it from him. Months before, I was so afraid of him, but he really has earned his way into my life. Do I have to be so afraid anymore? I don't know. I really would love to snack on those Gummy Bears before bed tonight. Maybe I should just take those and leave the rest, but, I have to admit, my first period was several weeks ago, and I sure was lonely and confused when I felt so achy and saw the blood. It was scary until it dawned on me what was going on. All the other girls I knew started their periods a long time ago, but I guess I sort of figured it wasn't going to happen to me. I couldn't ask Skip to buy anything like that. We would both die of embarrassment.

So, I guess I will swallow my pride and accept this stuff, but I want to pay her back the way I pay Skip back for the things he buys for me. I leaf through my notebook, tear out a page that features a nice drawing of leaves and one of the pond on the reverse, and leave it in the box. The other items are still in plastic shopping bags, so I heft them out and set back on my way retracing my steps.

On my walk back, heavily laden with treasures, I try to put myself in her shoes. Here she goes out in the woods and sees a girl dressed in oversized men's clothes getting water in jugs from the stream, and she sees this not once, like a kid going out from a campground to get water, but twice. She doesn't know that I'm not totally alone, in big trouble, in a tent somewhere. She is smart enough to figure out I'm hiding for some reason, and she doesn't want to scare me away. Skip had to approach me the same way, sort of like I was a wild animal. She obviously feels responsible for me, in some way—maybe because we are both women. Well, I guess we will have to see where this goes, if anywhere.

I arrive back home just as the sun is throwing long shadows through the pines. I gaze at the cold, colorful bottle of shampoo in my hand and am reminded of the "real" world I have abandoned for almost half a year…the people and the things I have left behind to focus on my survival. You would think I would be bored out here by myself, but, as the snow piles up around the cabin, even the sounds are keeping me company: the squeaking of the snow underfoot as I trudge out to the woodpile, the occasional muffled thud of snow sliding off pine boughs stirred by chilly breezes, the snap and crackle of the wood in my stove, coyotes singing at night, the boom coming from the pond as the thick ice expands and shifts.

My drawing pad is jammed full—fronts and backs of each page. I have taken to drawing small sketches in the margins, just little doodles that try to capture the essence of wood smoke, flame, snowfall, and the contours of snow as it is wind-carved into intricate shapes and drifts. I'm happy with some of these attempts. The doodles are quick and not fussy like some of my earlier drawings. The snow looks like clothes on fantasy creatures, and the tree stumps are garden gnomes with their stumpy, little bodies, big noses, and pointy hats. That is what is so cool about drawing; I find myself looking closely at even the smallest things I have never taken the time to notice.

Time is but the stream I go a-fishing in.   I drink at it; but while I drink I see the sandy bottom and detect how shallow it is. Its thin current slides away, but eternity remains. I would drink deeper; fish in the sky, whose bottom is pebbly with stars. I've got this saying and a drawing of the sandy bottom of my pond right next to where I carve my notches. I turned down Skip's offer of a little calendar he got in the mail. I really wouldn't need to go on with this morning ritual, but my notches are important to me. Each one reminds me of a day in my life that has counted for something. Henry reminds me that life is short—the stream is shallow—and it can't be wasted watching a clock. This is the first time in my life I have followed a schedule all my own; no alarm clock, no school bells ringing every 45 minutes moving me along with the herd from room to room, no life ruled by darkness and danger—in the impound lot by dark—off the streets after dark. Even when I was little I was commanded to leave my play to come in and get ready for bed—why? So I could do it all over again, and again, and again. I don't know how long this freedom can last, and it always is in the back of my brain that today could be the last day before my life changes, but I know now, no matter what happens tomorrow or the next day, I can be free and I will be free to live my own life.

Chapter 22

It's getting very close to Christmas, Skip tells me. He has already given me my wonderful fox fur hat and just last week taught me to make a new pair of deerskin choppers. I want to make something for him. I have to admit a sense of curiosity draws me toward the watering place today after three weeks of avoiding it thinking to discourage my mystery woman from seeking me out. I can't imagine she is willing to trudge out through this deep, deep snow, but I'll just give it a quick check for the heck of it.

As I approach, I can see where snowshoes and poles have made their way down the ridge and behind the beech tree. This woman must be as hard-headed as I am! The tracks are days old and have been snowed on, but the unmistakable beavertail shaped prints of snowshoes have created quite a distinct trail—a beaten path.

Before checking the cache, I think I will just trek up the ridge and see if I can figure out where she keeps coming from. A long forty-five minutes later, after traversing rough terrain and a stream, I emerge from the woods onto the side of a roadway—just a two-track like the lane to my cabin, but county plowed. The plow has mounded snow off to the side and created a little pull off. Snow tire tracks and the eroded remains of snowshoe prints. Okay, so now I know where she parks to get onto the trail. It's at least two miles in to the waterfall. She's a trooper—

must be young and healthy because I've worked up a pretty good sweat.

I return to the tree and brush a foot of fresh snow from the lid. I can't help but smile at the contents on top: granola bars, a solar-charged lantern that is really cool, a small mirror, a first aid kit with band aids and antiseptic cream, and a box of candy canes. I am speechless at what is packed in a bag at the bottom of the bin and only peek at the items. I cannot get them wet and snowy!

After hustling back to the cabin with wings on my feet, I shed my boots, coat, hat and choppers and stoke up the fire. I want to savor the gifts she has left for me. First, I unpack a set of twenty oil pastels, gorgeous colors of the rainbow. Next is a box of drawing pencils of different hardnesses and a sharpener. Some charcoals and soft white erasers and a couple of Pinkies are in a cookie tin. Finally, she has included three different pads of fine drawing paper: a little one to take in the field for sketches, another for medium sized layouts and small drawings, and the last is serious paper—big and beautiful for use with pencil and pastels for some truly finished pieces of real art. I bring the paper to my nose and inhale. I hug the small sketchpad to my chest. I am ready for this—somehow she knows.

The wonderful texture of the creamy white paper and the kaleidoscope of pastel colors speak of spring, summer, and fall. I am truly touched by the kindness of this person and quietly whisper my thanks. I feel as if my life has been given a lift—a new beginning—as the passion for creating art has been growing slowly and steadily throughout my time of isolation. It all feels purposeful, and I have never felt purposeful before. *Thank you. Truly thank you, whoever you are. Merry Christmas!*

Chapter 23

205 notches! Skip is coming over for Christmas today. He is bringing canned venison and potatoes to bake in the coals, and I'm baking a dried apple and berry crisp for dessert in my iron skillet. I got the recipe from *Mother Earth News.* An awesome aroma is filling the cabin, and the crisp is beginning to bubble, the oatmeal topping turning a golden brown. Yum! My cabin is so warm and steamy I can't see out any of the windows, but I hear the crunch of snow and the familiar, "Hello in the house!"

"Hey, Skippy!"

"Hey, kid! Merry Christmas! I brought the grub. I'm ready to stuff myself and annihilate you at poker. I'm sorry you're such a fast learner, though. Mmmm…somethin' sure smells good!"

Skip is amazed when I show him the art supplies my mystery woman left for me.

"Huh. Wonder who she is?"

"Seriously…you don't know, do you?"

"Honest, Jenna. I'm startin' to have a suspicion, but I'm not positive who is doin' this."

"Will you help me figure it out?"

"Well, I'm okay with keepin' my eyes and ears open when I'm in town, but you need to think about it before you decide if you want to have another person know where you are and who you are since you are still a minor."

"Yeah, I guess you are right. I'd be in a mess if the cops would turn up in the middle of the winter.

Let's see if Mystery Woman keeps this up. Maybe she'll get bored with me. It's costing her a lot of money to buy this stuff for me. She must be rich. Wonder what she wants from me?"

"Maybe nothin', Jenna. Maybe she's just a carin' person."

"About someone she doesn't even know?"

"Yep. There are folks like that, dontcha know. Actually, more in the UP than anywhere else I've ever been."

"Guess so. We'll see."

"Anyhow, shuffle those cards, eh. Let's have a game while the potatoes bake. I'm going to kick your butt! And then we'll eat!"

Chapter 24

The January thaw has come and gone and bone-chilling cold has followed for several weeks on and off in February, March, and April, but now the ice is finally receding from the margins of the pond. The remaining ice is gray and pockmarked. I saw a river otter yesterday climb out of a hole in the ice and feast on a big perch. After he left the skeletal remains of the fish, a bald eagle swooped down onto the ice and finished it off. It's the beginning of May. I've been here eleven months and can't wait for the first bits of green to appear. I've been trying to work with my pastels in spring colors, but they are just not right. Everything looks too green in my drawings, like I'm looking through weird-tinted, green lenses. I need to see the real thing: some cattail shoots, the little buds on the maples, the early trillium and Dutchman's breeches in the woods. The wild leeks—or ramps—taste like strong onions, and I'm looking forward to adding a couple of them into a fish dinner. I've missed eating fish this winter. Skip offered to teach me how to ice fish but that sounded like a boring, brutal time with cold feet just to pull a couple of little perch out of a hole. No, thanks! I would rather be here by my woodstove working on my drawings and eating corncakes, rice, and beans.

The Mystery Woman has fallen into a once a month delivery routine since before Christmas, and she has me caught hook, line, and sinker, as Uncle Bill would say. She has brought me more shampoo and conditioner, two books about art: one on pastel techniques which I have been studying and one entitled *Drawing the Head and Hands* by Andrew Loomis. It's an old copy, with a couple of pages loose, notes in the margins, and pages dog-eared. There is a clue to her identity in it, though. The title page has an inscription: To Carol from Charles, Christmas 1968. Her name may be Carol, or this is a thrift shop find. I'm not very interested in portraits, but I have tried a couple of self-portrait sketches looking into the mirror. It's kind of fun to really, really study my eyes and try to capture the shape and expression in them. I never really knew how my features all work together in proportion. My nose is weird. All noses are weird.

Each time the woman has left something for me, I have paid her with a drawing. In February, the cache contained an envelope on top of her gifts. Inside were two twenty dollar bills! I thought at first she was just going to start giving me money, and I was determined not to accept it, but then I read her note:

Hello. I hope it was okay to show your drawings to a friend. I told her they were drawn by a neighbor of mine—no more details than that. She sells gifts and cards in her bookshop in Marquette, and she asked if two of them were for sale. I think I negotiated a pretty good price for you. She would like to have a few more, if you are willing. Just let me know if I'm out of line. If you leave more drawings, I will presume it is okay to sell them for you. If not, I'll know you are not interested.

Skip thinks I can take her at her word. When I showed him the name on the flyleaf of the portrait book, I saw a glimmer of recognition in his eyes. I think he knows who Mystery Woman is, but so far he's not telling, and I am not asking. This arrangement is working out without complicating my good life here, so far. I have paid Skip everything I owe him and have $40 in my Jordan payback fund in my glove box bank. I'm just going to let it be and continue to take it one day at a time.

Chapter 25

I awake to the sound of shattering glass. Oh, no! Someone is breaking into the car. *Mom, Mom! Watch out! Get out!* But, no—I'm in the pitch dark in a cellar—my cellar—my root cellar. What is that awful noise? I hear wood splintering and shuffling footsteps above me on the cabin floor and a snuffling and muffled growl that can only mean one thing—bear! OMG! *Wake up, Jenna!* It's right over my head on the trapdoor, and it must be big because the door is flexing with its weight. I click on the solar lantern and begin to scream, "Get out of here you stupid, stupid bear!" I scream over and over until my throat is raw. I bang my cooking pot and lid together. "Go away! Go away! Please, go away!" Black bears usually will do anything to avoid human contact, but I am down here with all this food, and this guy is just out of winter sleep and starving.

My shouts discourage him for a minute, and I keep still and hope for the best, but he returns. The trapdoor is sagging under his weight and claws are scraping and prying again. The growling gets louder and more threatening. He's not messing around. I dress quickly and roughly move things around to make room to climb up the shelving to reach my escape vent. *I can do this. Stay calm, Jenna.* I dig into the chest and grab the rifle and ammunition from the bottom. My fingers are shaking violently as I try to load the bullets the way I watched Skip load his rifle. I don't want to kill this thing. I don't know if I even *can* kill this thing with this gun, but I'm going to go down fighting with all I've got, if he traps me down here.

The plywood is splintering. It's only going to be seconds until the bear breaks through and will fall down on top of me! I hoist the rifle onto the highest shelf and begin my climb—bottom shelf, second shelf. I clutch the sharp metal supports feeling no pain, and adrenaline carries me onto the top shelf, panting and in a panic. I pry off the vent cover and shove the rifle through the hole, easing myself through behind. My belt and knife catch on the frame, but I manage to reach around and free myself. I fall onto my hands and knees in the shallow crawl space under the cabin. The solar lantern has dropped onto the cellar floor, illuminating the space, but putting me out here in the dark. I wham my head on a floor joist hard enough to see stars. I go down on my elbows and scoot to turn around.

I watch, holding my breath, shivering, as the bear finally dislodges the trapdoor from its hinges and shards of plywood angle down with a crash into the space. He is hanging his big, black head down into the cellar. OMG, his shaggy head is huge! He growls and I see his yellowed teeth and smell his rank breath. I feel like puking. His head swings back and forth, nervously scanning the cellar space. He is hesitating because in order to get the food he is going to have to jump and there is no clear way out for him once he is down in the cellar. The ladder is jammed behind the trapdoor. His desperation for food and his instinct for survival are battling: stomach versus brain.

It's now or never for me. I take a long, shuddering breath. Dang it! He's in MY house and after MY food! His size gave him the first advantage, but I have the advantage now with firepower. I recall the sound of Skip's shot in the deer blind. I aim to put the fear of God into this creature. He's too big to get into this shallow crawl space, so I am safe under the cabin. I poke the muzzle of the rifle through the vent, snap off the safety, and wait until he pulls his head back out of the way.

BOOM! The sound of my shot kills my ears, but I hear the bear bawl with fear and surprise. BLAM!, the gun recoils painfully against my shoulder, and again, BOOM! I am deafened, but feel the actual vibration in the floor above me as he begins to run frantically around the cabin, crashing into everything and violently forcing his way out. I turn and see his shadow as he barrels past the woodpile and crashes into the woods, running for his life.

Collapsing onto my side in the cold dirt, I curl up, and will myself to breathe again. My ears are painfully ringing and my eyes and mouth are full of grit from the explosions. The whole experience seems like a nightmare, but I know it has been real because the cold is overcoming the numbness and shock and my toes are freezing. I realize I have no boots on my feet—no hat, coat, or gloves, either—but I have my life. I protected MY house and MY food all by myself, bravely and without hesitation.

I'm not one of those movie females who stand by while others take what is hers, no! I'll keep what's mine, come hell or high water. Right now, though, I need to stay put to make sure the bear is long gone.

I pull my long pant legs over my feet, and my long sleeves over my hands, and stay still in the crawl space. I may have even dozed a little bit in the early dawn light. I'm just rousing myself from my stupor when I hear Skip barging down the trail, *swish, thump, swish, thump*! Breathlessly he shouts, "Jenna, Jenna. Are you all right? Where are you? Talk to me!!"

"Skip, I'm down under here." In a moment, a wide-eyed, frantic face is peering into the crawl space.

"I heard shots! What is goin' on here, eh? Are you okay?"

"Yeah. Bear."

"Bear?"

"Uh huh. He broke into the cabin, smashed the trap door and was going to get into my root cellar. I squeezed out here through a vent and shot at him." I started wearily to crawl toward him on elbows and knees. I'm tired—so tired.

"Did ya kill him?"

"Naw. He ran off. Hey, would you go in and get me my boots from beside the stove?"

Skip hustles off, returns, and tosses me my boots. I pull them on and he helps haul me and the rifle out from under the cabin and onto my feet.

"It's pretty bad messed up in there, Jenna. Stinks like bear, too."

"Yeah? Dang."

"Well, I'll bet that bear will run all the way to the Mackinac Bridge! You won't see him around here again. Let's get you inside. I'll stir up the stove and put on the coffeepot. Tell me all about it while you warm up. Geez, kid! Didn't know you had it in you! You've got sisu. Remind me never to tangle with you!" I can see pride and relief in his eyes.

"See soo, what's that?"

"It's spelled s i s u. Sisu. I grew up with my grandparents talkin' about it. It's the best thing a person can have. It is the Finnish idea of courage—more than courage—guts. When you can face a challenge with smarts and bravery and never give up. The greatest compliment I ever got was when my dad sent me out alone to get my second deer. I shot a nice doe and field dressed it just as he had taught me. When I came back with the heart, liver, draggin' a back quarter, he clapped me on the back and told me, 'Kid, you got sisu. It's getting' dark, so you lead me back there and I'll help you bring the rest of it out of the woods.' My feet never touched the ground as we walked back there, side by side—his hand on my shoulder."

Sisu. Even though my cabin was a stinky mess and repairs took us all day, I never smiled so much in my life.

Chapter 26

One attraction in coming to the woods to live was that I should have leisure and opportunity to see the spring come in. The ice in the pond at length begins to be honey-combed, and I can set my heel in it as I walk. Fogs and rains and warmer suns are gradually melting the snow; the days have grown sensibly longer; and I see how I shall get through the winter without adding to my wood-pile, for large fires are no longer necessary.

A soft musical whistle, the flutter of light gray wings, and a scolding *churr churr churr* fill the air. The little beggar is back for the second time today for her dried apple treats. A stylish little bird adorned with blue-gray feathers lands lightly on the woodpile. Now, she's strutting up and down demanding a second helping and scolds me as I carefully approach with hand outstretched. I remember these birds of the northern forest are called gray jays.

"You will only get an apple slice if you take it from my hand today, Sisu. C'mon. You know me and don't have to be afraid."

She cocks her head to the side to look me over. Her black eyes give her an intense look, as if she wishes she could knock me down and take the apple by force, but she is a smart little gal. I have watched her use a stick as a tool to pry rice kernels out of the woodpile when they slip out of reach of her beak. She thinks things through, and she is carefully considering if hunger is strong enough to overcome her fears.

I slowly wave the apple to entice her to land on my arm. We have played this game every day for the past two weeks, and I can see her resolve is weakening and her trust is growing. She finally makes up her mind, takes a big hop and swoop, brushes my arm with her wings, and grabs the apple from my fingers. She doesn't land, but that it is progress. I've heard that with patience, you can teach some birds to talk. That would be cool. So far, I haven't taught her to talk, but she has taught me her soft whistle and she definitely knows her name and will come when I call, as long as there is a food reward.

Green is popping out all over by the pond and cabin. This is an earlier than usual spring this year, for which Skip and I are grateful. He says we are about two weeks ahead of most years, and the woods has sent up the first spring beauties and jacks in the pulpit are scattered all about. Leeks are filling the woods—trillium and morel mushrooms not far behind. One full cycle. I shake my head and smile in disbelief.

Mystery Woman has been faithful. Since our first contact last December, she has made a monthly trek out to the cache. She has left more art supplies and things a girl needs to feel like a girl even if she is wearing men's long drop butt underwear, flannel, and wool. A hand knit toboggan cap and scarf were in the March box; someone is very talented. The colors are wonderful greens and rusts and mahogany like the fall woods. The scarf has a thin line of blue like a stream running through it. Gorgeous! She has sold four more of my drawings—one was a pastel of an inside scene of the cabin that featured the two chair quotation by Thoreau. I have saved seven $20 bills in my bank. My pastel work is getting better and I am out today trying to capture the essence of the early spring colors and shapes around the pond. Before, I would have claimed that grass is green, water is blue, and the clouds are white, but I can see how ignorant that was. Close observation allows me to use almost all the pastels in my box in one way or other to capture the spring day. The blending sticks fine-tune my colors, and I have spent many evenings studying color theory from the books. It's awesome to learn all of this and then be able to go out and accomplish just what I envision.

I grab my gallon jugs and roll up several of my best drawings to check out the cache today. It's a beautiful, sunny day with a breeze from the south warming and melting off the last bits of snow and ice from the shadiest places. I'm in no particular rush today, and so when I get to the watering place, I sit back on a rock, enjoy the sound of the splashing, and watch some crawdads trying to keep from getting washed away in the current. They feel their way in the shallows like baby lobsters. The water is lovely and hypnotizing.

Suddenly, I hear a soft, high voice and lift my head to listen. I may be mistaken. The musical sound may be the water playing over and around the rocks, but I hear it again.

"Please don't be afraid."

My first thought is to jump up and run, but she has me at a disadvantage sitting down here by the stream. The voice is coming from the cache. Slowly, something much like a Hobbit emerges from behind the tree. This fantasy vision wears a heavy green coat with peaked hood hiding her face except for a pair of bright eyes behind round glasses. Her woolen pants are tucked into tall leather boots, and she carries a crooked walking staff. The tiny being approaching is something from a British novel come to life: a woods creature from a mossy glen. I realize my mouth is hanging open in surprise and clamp it shut.

"Hello there. Name's Carol. I didn't come here on purpose to meet you—didn't expect to see you." The sound of a soft, gentle woman's voice sounds foreign to my ears. It has been a long time since anyone approached me with such kind and loving words. I am spellbound.

"Hello," I manage, as I rise from the rock and face her square on. I tower over her.

She slips off the hood, revealing a head of short, curly, gray hair. There is a spring in her step as she approaches me, and she is coming faster than I would like. OMG, she looks like a hugger! Like some sort of grandma hugger! I take several awkward steps backward, and she slows her pace. I am steeling for an embrace from this stranger, ready to squeeze my eyes shut and endure it, but, to my surprise, she merely extends her hand and smiles a lovely, open smile.

Her hand is warm and soft, but her handshake firm and her touch sends a shiver up my arm. I feel a blush coming to my cheeks. The contact is pleasant and comforting. I realize in a rush of emotion just how much I have missed a woman's touch. After we shake hands, I jam mine into my pockets and look down. My thoughts are whirling. *Where is this conversation going to go? Jenna, keep your head.*

She motions me to sit with her and the rock ledge necessitates that we sit close together. She doesn't look me in the eye, but allows the flowing water to play around the tip of her walking stick. It gives us both something to look at as we begin to talk.

"I have been thinking about you so much every day. It takes a lot of bravery to be by yourself for so long, but you look as if you are managing okay. I was hoping we could visit face-to-face one day."

"I have wondered about you, too. Thanks for all the gifts—especially the art stuff. You didn't have to do that."

"I knew any kindness would not be wasted on you. Somehow I sensed that the first time I saw you. I am amazed at the improvement in your sketches in just the little time you have been sharing them with me. You are very talented. I would like to call you by your name. Would you share that, as well?"

"Jenna."

"Beautiful name for a beautiful young woman. Jenna. Finnish?"

"I was named for my grandmother whose parents came from Finland." Mom had told me that once upon a time.

"The Finns have made a wonderful contribution to the UP. You come from good stock, you know." She glanced over at the drawings. "Well, Jenna. I see you have brought some art for the cache today. May I see your drawings?"

I bring over the pastels. She holds out her hands to receive them with a delighted look on her face, handling them as if they are precious.

"What have we here? Oh, spring colors on the forest floor with a background of budding birch trees. Well done! I can just hear the music of the woods in this pastel. Will you also be trying to capture this little waterfall in color?"

"I've been thinking about it, but I can't seem to get the colors right on the water."

"Water is tough, but you will catch on to it. Do a lot of small experiments on your paper. There is plenty more where that came from, so use it up! Actually, you caught me leaving more supplies for you."

"This is costing you a fortune....um...Carol."

"Pish tosh. I'm making an investment in you, Jenna. Worth every penny. Don't give it another thought. Is it okay for me to keep selling your work? My friend in Marquette is always glad to see me come in the door. You should see her smile! I'm going to get you more for these pastels, you just wait and see."

She laughs a birdlike, musical laugh. I can't help but smile.

"Okay, but please do something for me. Take whatever you spend for the supplies out of that money, okay? I don't like to owe anyone anything. It would sure make me feel better."

She didn't hesitate one moment. "Okay. It's a deal! Want to try acrylic on canvas sometime just for fun? I hope so, because in the cache you're going to find some brushes, small canvases and some paints this time. Good for abstract work. Let's take a look."

She leads the way behind the beech tree. In the container are tubes of paints, a variety of brushes, a palette, canvas boards of different sizes, and Oreos double wrapped in plastic and foil so a bear can't smell them, she explained. The bags also hold canned peaches and pears, toilet paper, and my monthly supply of pads. My face warms when I draw out this package, and she notices my discomfort.

"I keep buying those for you because I figure that wouldn't have been something you would have thought to pack when you came to stay, and they are a necessity at your age. I'm delighted to say I don't need them anymore. The checkout person probably wonders why an 80 year old is buying them every month!" She laughs that infectious laugh again, and I chuckle quietly, too.

"Well, I have more calls to make today, but I'm sure glad we ran into each other and, even more wonderful to know your name, Jenna. Goodbye for now. You are a bright, capable young woman. I hope we can be friends."

This time there is a goodbye hug—warm, all encompassing, and tender. I feel myself melt into her arms, giving and receiving the embrace equally. Had no idea I missed that so much. I watch her walk away, but not back the way she came. She carefully fords the stream using the walking stick to balance and makes her way on an almost invisible trail to my right. I watch her as she waves over her shoulder before disappearing into the woods, and I listen as the happy tune she is humming fades away.

Chapter 27

"O.K. Skip, tell me. Who is she?"

"You mean Carol?"

"Yes. You have known for a couple of months now, haven't you?"

"Yeah, I was pretty sure your Mystery Woman was the preacher lady."

"Preacher lady?"

"Yep. She is in charge of the little Presbyterian Church in Birch Bay—been there quite a few years now. Fine person. Her congregation relies on her and she's sort of a one woman show for those folks. I've had her stop by my cabin once or twice as she goes on her rounds, and I consider her one of my few friends."

"Rounds?"

"Yeah, she kind of keeps tabs on the population of those of us who make ourselves scarce in town and live off the land—self-reliant folks like me and you."

"Well, I sure as heck don't want her preaching at me."

"No worries. She's the truest person of God I've ever met."

"What do you mean by that?"

"I'll let you figure it out as you get to know her, but you can trust her with your life. I do. She's got sisu, too."

Chapter 28

365 notches! My anniversary of life at Loon Haven. I wake up in my tent on the porch, stretch as tall as I can in the sunshine, and look out at the loons playing on the pond. Last year I arrived scared, friendless, broke, orphaned, brokenhearted, and homeless. Now I am confident in my survival skills, have two friends and a pet wild bird, a growing pile of $20 bills in the glove box, and a pretty comfortable home. I've learned to fish, cook, field dress a deer, draw in perspective, use charcoals, work with pastels, and I'm beginning to figure out how to handle acrylic paints. I've fought off a bear, gathered enough wood for two winters, and learned to run a woodstove without burning down my cabin.

Last week, I decided to leave a map to my cabin and an invitation to Carol in the cache. Someday before too long I expect I will have a visitor. It has been impossible to forget that hug, and, frankly, I feel the need for more human contact. Skip is my best buddy and always will be, but that brief visit with another woman left me wanting more: more of her genuine interest in me just the way I am, another chance to talk about art and show her my work, another one of those comforting hugs. So, today, I am tidying up. I gather all my scattered artwork that is in different stages of completion and put it in a sort of viewing order. The pastel book featured a beautiful waterlily print by a fellow named Monet. I studied the way he handled the water and tried to copy some of those shapes and colors. It is a good first try, and I want to show it to Carol. Skip likes it, but he likes anything I do. I think she would be willing to be more critical and give me her honest opinion and maybe some pointers about how I can improve.

"Hello in the house!" A familiar voice calls out.

"Hi, Skippy! You sound cheerful. What's up?"

"Well, let me show you this!" From behind his back, he pulls out his dripping fish stringer. He has managed to catch a huge pike. Its gray-green and deep blue scales glisten in the sun. An impossible number of wicked teeth gleam, needle-like, from its evil, gaping jaws.

"Wow! What a fish!"

"Had a battle with this fellow, dontcha know. I thought I was hooked on a log on the bottom until he started to slowly move. He let me pull him up, looked me right in the eye, and then took off pullin' and zigzaggin' like mad. Pretty good catch on light tackle, eh? Want me to cook him up here for a little shore lunch?"

"Sure. I'm pretty hungry. Just toss the guts on that wild rose over there and get a fire going. I'll get an onion and some of those potatoes you brought me last week and the skillet and some oil."

We both get to work and soon the wonderful aroma of fried fish, onions, and potatoes sprinkled liberally with salt and pepper fills the air around the campfire. As we settle onto our accustomed stump seats, we begin to eat in friendly silence. Skip is the master of comfortable silences. When I asked him about that, he says his father despised chatter and would leave the room and go split wood when the ladies would go to gossiping or the men talking politics. He spoke seldom, but when he did, people listened. His words were straight forward and gruff, but he said what he was really thinking, and he didn't beat around the bush. That is the Finnish way. Skip said I would find that was a part of the Yooper culture.

"Skip, I've noticed you don't sound like my Uncle Bill when you talk."

He takes time to put his empty plate down, knocks out his pipe bowl and loads it with fresh tobacco from his pouch. He lights his pipe with a smoldering stick from the campfire, and stretches out his feet toward the fire. He is a man of few words, but I know the signs he's about to tell a story. I have come to recognize his wind up like the pitcher in a baseball game.

"When I was in boot camp in Parris Island, it suited me just fine to say 'YES, SIR!' a million times a day—and to fall into my bunk at night exhausted without speakin' to anyone. I didn't have time to talk, or think, or dwell on the past. But one day I was ordered to explain somethin' from the trainin' manual. When I opened my mouth and my UP accent came out, the commander gave out an explosive laugh; even my friends in the platoon smirked. I was humiliated. My commander was from Connecticut and had an accent I found odd and hard to understand, but, for some reason, the way I spoke seemed comical to everyone."

"How come?"

"Well, Mom used to tell me that the Finns came to the UP to mine and work the timber late in the 1800's. Later, when the mines played out and the virgin forest was cut down, they raised strawberries and potatoes on the land that had been cleared. They could all read, write and speak in Finnish—were well educated before they came to the US—but didn't know English, which is a very different language in sounds and structure. When they got here they grouped up, lived close together, established cooperatives for shoppin', and had newspapers and church services in Finnish, so there wasn't much of a reason for the women, especially, to learn English. The workin' men picked up English slowly for their jobs so they could understand the crew leader's orders, but they didn't practice it much among themselves, and so their bosses thought they were stupid and backward, even though they might have had more schoolin' than anyone on the job. It came to be that if you spoke Finnglish, as they call it, you were automatically considered backward, rural, and poor—and a reason to make fun. You know, Jenna, you have an accent, too. There's somethin' about the Hoosier way of draggin' out your vowels and using old timey expressions that marks you as different, too."

"Really? I never thought of that. Guess I picked up my way of talking from my grandparents when I was really little."

"Probably. So, after many years in the Marines, I began pick up a mutt-sort of accent. I can still use my Finnglish if I want—sort of like a second language. 'Say yah to da UP, eh.'" He chuckles. "When I'm in town around the fellas I can turn it on. When I'm with you, I pretty much turn it off. Make sense?"

"Sure does. Another thing. Uncle Bill didn't like to be called a Yooper. How about you?"

"Heck, Yooper wasn't even a word until the 70's. Some people are proud to be everything Yooper stands for: independent, resilient, brave—sisu. Others think it is an insult and don't find a lot of humor in the stereotype of the backwoods, deer camp, pasty-eatin', beer-drinkin' man walkin' around his house and splittin' wood in his union suit and blaze orange cap. Many of our grandpas and dads were part of that culture, though, and, even though our English teachers taught us their grammar was wrong and made them sound ignorant, we loved and respected them as hard-workin', God-fearin', patriotic men. We knew each man truly deserved his week off at deer camp in November, and his winter Sundays in the icehouse catchin' perch while snackin' on a big ring of bologna and a six pack of beer. Those few days weren't a 24/7 way of life for a UP man, but looked forward to as a rare chance to relax, rest his tired body, and use his skills to feed his family, socialize, and have some good-natured fun. My dad did backbreakin' work in the timber all his life, but he lived for those days of huntin' and fishin'. I fit pretty square in the Yooper culture, so I don't mind. Call me anythin', just call me." His laugh rang out across the pond.

"I get it now. Thanks."

"Well, gotta get home and feed the chickens. Will you clean up?"

"Sure. Thanks for sharing the fish, and for talking."

"Before you came, it was years since I put a string of words together like this. I'm kinda rusty."

"Naw. You make me feel at home here. You—and Henry. And Sisu."

"Sisu?"

"Watch this. I holler 'Sisu, come here!' Like magic, my little gray jay appears from behind the cabin, swoops over Skip's head, spreads her wings, and lands gracefully on my outstretched arm. I feed her a morsel of fish, and she responds with a satisfied soft whistle. Skip's eyes and delighted laugh warm my heart as Sisu dances up and down my forearm and finally settles up on my shoulder, playfully pecking and tugging at my collar for another treat.

"Well, that beats all. I'm leavin' you in good company, Jenna." He waved bye and headed off into the woods. *Swish, thump, swish, thump.*

Chapter 29

A lake is a landscape's most beautiful and expressive feature. It is Earth's eye; looking into which the beholder measures the depth of his own nature. Earth's eye. It's so true. It's finally warm enough to take my first swim of the summer today, and as I reach the middle of the pond, I am reminded of these words. I take a deep breath, lay my head back and extend my arms to float outstretched in the chilly water. Cold water rushes into my ears and brushes my lips as I gaze skyward. My hair fans out around my head and shoulders, and I am weightless. This pond is an eye and I am its pupil. The eye gazes into the sky, and I become part of the great, blue, cloudless infinity. My only sensation is listening to my steady, slow heartbeat magnified by my submerged ears. My mind empties of all thoughts. I am suspended in space, totally at peace.

A cool breeze on my face finally interrupts my daydreams. I flip over to swim back and steel myself to loon dive under the surface where the layers of water are colder the further down I go. My eyeballs ache underwater, but I want to see the sandy, weedy bottom below me—minnows dashing away, rocks covered with algae and fish eggs, a little perch hanging on the bottom willing itself to be invisible. I surface, take a big breath, and dive back down again braving the coldest water near the bottom. The perch panics and scoots off with a flash of his silver tail. Water weeds, some like thickly furred raccoon tails and others like spindly vines, tangle on the bottom and rise up to the light. Waterlily stems reach toward the surface, leaves unfurling into round floating rafts for the frogs, turtles, and dragonflies to rest upon.

After my swim, I towel off with an old tee shirt. The sun is warm and I sit for a while in my underwear that substitutes for a bikini. This afternoon, I will wash my winter clothes in my tree trunk sink, hang them to dry, and pack them away. I still have a few summer clothes that fit: two tee shirts, a pair of sweatpants, and plastic flip flops for my feet around camp. As long as I can toss a flannel shirt over my tee shirt when I hear Skip's hello in the house, I don't really need a bra—not going to be one of those D cup girls, for sure, and that's a-ok with me!

My clean sweatpants and tee shirt feel great. Just as I plunge my trusty union suit into my makeshift sink bubbly with castile soap, I hear a musical, "Hello there! Okay to come on?"

"Yes." My heart skips a beat. Here I go. This is a big step in an uncertain direction. *It's okay, Jenna. She is little and old. You can always outrun her if things get weird.*

Carol steps into view and approaches on the pond trail. She is in jeans, boots, and a navy sweatshirt that says Northern Michigan University on the front, a baseball cap taming her curly hair. Walking stick in her right hand. Even in her summer gear, she looks kinda like a gnome. She stops and takes in my camp from a distance: the cabin, the outhouse, my wet, winter clothes draped over the woodpile, and then she smiles.

"This is just as I had envisioned your camp would be, Jenna. Thanks for inviting me. Hope today's okay." She took a substantial pack off her shoulders and swung it onto the ground with a thump. This woman says she is in her 80's, but it is super hard to believe.

"Sure. I'm just doing my laundry here."

"Don't let me stop you. You gotta get it done while your water's hot enough to do the trick. I'll just park myself over here and keep you company for a bit."

"Okay. This is the last of it."

"You sure have a pretty spot here, Jenna. Right on the pond and all."

"Yeah, I really like it."

"Looks like you have been working hard to get a wood supply and make improvements to your cabin."

"It isn't much, but it was a real mess when I got here, for sure."

I rinse out my union suit, wring it out, and drape it over the woodpile.

"There. I'm done. Thought it was time to finally get out my summer clothes."

"I did the same thing yesterday—hand washed my gray long johns."

"You wear long johns, too?"

"Oh, yeah! They are the greatest invention in the world."

"Ha. My uncle used to say the same thing."

I realize I need to shut up and not give out too much information to this woman. She holds the upper hand over me no matter how friendly and nice. I lower my eyes. This may be trouble. She senses my hesitation and fear.

"Jenna, I am good for my word. Let's get that straight. I will not tell anyone you are here unless your life is in danger. That promise will stand until you tell me otherwise, okay? Pinky swear?"

I take a deep breath. "Okay." I look into her sincere blue eyes. Neither of us looks away for a long moment. She extends her hand, palm down, little finger extended. I haven't done this ritual since I was seven years old on the playground. We link pinky fingers and laugh at our silliness. Promise made.

"I'd love a cabin tour. Do you have time to show me around? I have already seen your outhouse—super charming," she laughs that musical laugh, and I have to join her. The tension is broken between us. She swings her backpack up off the ground onto her shoulder.

"Got a few things here to share with you. Let's unpack 'em inside."

I'm excited to see her reaction to my house and watch her carefully as she slowly takes everything in with as much interest as if she is visiting a mansion. She comments on how smart it is to pitch my tent on the porch and says she wishes she had a screened in porch at her house. She runs her hand over some of my notches without comment, but I know she recognizes them for what they are. My stove wood wall impresses her, but the thing that stops her in her tracks is the artwork I have chosen to hang on my walls. She slowly circles the room studying each drawing, pastel, or painting in turn. I watch her pleasant but impassive face as she steps forward and then back to consider each work—a critical but loving dance. She spots the pile of paper on the floor.

"Oh, you are putting together a portfolio! May I take a look?"

This is what I have been waiting for. She sits in Skip's chair and extends her hands as if she is getting ready to hold someone's precious child in her arms. I pull my chair next to hers and we spend time talking about each piece. We both can see how much my work has progressed as we look at them, one by one.

"The instruction books you put in the cache have been great. I love filling the long hours of my life here with art. There is something in it that does my heart good and makes me feel free and connected. It takes loneliness away."

"I get it, Jenna. No one can take your creative freedom away from you, and you are finding your voice through your art. You are young to be living this solitary life. Most women couldn't be making their way out here. There is something special and wonderful about you. The Finns would say you have sisu. Do you know that word?"

I smile. "Yes, I do. Thank you. It is a great compliment."

She suddenly claps her hands and smiles, "Let's pretend it is Christmas. Unpack Santa's bag, ok?" She chuckles.

Can all women read each other's minds? A fabric bag full of spring clothes from a resale shop includes two pairs of khaki shorts, several tee shirts, Nike tennis shoes that look like a perfect fit, and light socks. She has included a one piece swimsuit with red and green stripes. I pull out a package of new underpants, toiletries, and more art supplies. Three more twenty dollar bills are in an envelope.

"I did as you asked and took out all my costs, Jenna. We are totally square. Before I forget, I want to know if there is anything I can do for you that is hard for you to accomplish from out here."

This was an opportunity I had not considered. "Maybe there is something, Carol. One of my friends lent me some money to get up here, and paying him back has been on my mind."

"Want me to get in touch with him?"

I give her the name and general location of the restaurant and ask her to call them and leave her phone number for Jordan.

"He's a neat person and will be very relieved to hear from you. I want to be able to write to him and let him know I'm okay. Maybe you could figure out how to turn my $20 bills into a money order or something to send to him. I don't know how to do that."

"Sure. My bank in Marquette will help me with that when we get an address for your friend and you have time to write to him. May take me a while to do this, okay?"

"No prob."

I walk her out of the cabin. She has three of my best spring pastels safely wrapped and stowed in the fabric bag. We share a warm hug, and for fun I call "Sisu, come here!" Again, out of the pines, swoops my loyal, little friend. She makes her alarm sounds at the sight of a stranger, *Chee, chee, chee!*

"It's ok, Sisu. Come." Carol's eyes light up as the little bird lands on my arm to get a bit of cornbread I saved for her. She dances and struts up and down my arm, making her soft whistle—really putting on a show.

"What a delight! I'm so glad to have a friend like you, Jenna. Bye for now. I may not get all the way to the cabin to see you for a while, but check on our cache. That trail's on my monthly calling route. Leave a message, if you need help with anything or if you want to meet by the waterfall."

"Bye, Carol. Thanks for everything. I really mean it."

As Sisu perches on my shoulder, Carol turns on her heel, waves over her shoulder, and heads around the pond. I stand still and listen hard until her happy humming fades away.

I get out my copy of *Walden* and turn to a passage that Uncle Bill underlined with pencil and I've been puzzling over. *Why should we be in such desperate haste to succeed, and in such desperate enterprises? If a man does not keep pace with his companions, perhaps it is because he hears a different drummer. Let him step to the music which he hears, however measured or far away.* I'm beginning to understand that Skip, Carol and I each travel to the beat of our own drummer—and I like the beat I hear. It is obvious, the more I get to know these two friends, they do, too. "I have two friends and you, little bird." I tell Sisu. She whistles in agreement and flies into the pines. Now, let's try on these new clothes!

Chapter 30

Ouch, ouch, ouch!! The UP is famous for no-see-ums, blackflies, mosquitoes, deerflies, horseflies, and stable flies that can ruin whole weeks at a time. Mosquito repellent works on mosquitoes, but the others seem to thrive on licking the repellent off your skin before they BITE—and BITE HARD! Black flies swoop into your eyes, fly up your nose, burrow into your ears, and stroll down the part in your hair, taking big bites all the way, and hunker down in all the nooks and crannies of your neck. The only way to survive a couple hours fishing is to tuck your long pants into your socks, button up a dark colored long sleeve shirt—never light blue—and put on a wide brimmed hat with a head net over it tied at your collar. Skip lent me a hat and head net, and they have been lifesavers. Your exposed hands just have to deal with multiple, painful bites because insect repellent is murder on fishing gear—eats it right up—and the fish are disgusted with it, too. Geez! No wonder the people are so tough up here! Sheila of the high school bully squad would love this! Ha.

Another 4th of July is here and another birthday with it. I'm 16 today and somehow feel lots older than I did yesterday. I braved the daytime blackflies to get some campfire wood together earlier, and now I am intentionally sitting exactly where I was last year at this time. I hear the sporadic fireworks booming in the distance on this still night. The bugs have let up as darkness has arrived, thank goodness. A squadron of ghostly moths fly in and out of the campfire light. Once in a while one makes a misjudgment and sizzles in the coals. It is interesting how living things are attracted to heat and light. I'll have to see if Henry says anything about that in his book. Seems like something he would wonder about, too.

In this last year, I have endured a long winter even though Skip tells me I got off easy with less snow and warmer temps than usual. I think a super thing about this year is how I am getting so much better at looking at things, not just how the world hits my eyes, but how the colors and shapes work together to make up all of nature—how the colors blend or clash, how the shapes are so beautiful, how water, air, and fire are life. Most importantly, I have made and kept two friends—more than friends. I have a new family. I feel equal with these special people. I've noticed Skip doesn't call me 'kid' anymore. It feels so good for the days to flow by. I'm growing inside and outside and respecting and being respected. *Thank you, Uncle Bill, for Loon Haven and teaching me to care. Thank you, Mom, for your lessons about strength and weakness. Thank you, Skip, for your encouragement and friendship, and thanks, Carol, for coming into my life just when I needed purpose.*

The cache contained Jordan's address last time I went for water in June. She got it somehow. After the coals burn down to a weak glow, I pour water over the fire, stir the still-smoking embers, and head back to the porch. I light the lantern, get out paper and pen and settle down to write my first communication to the outside world after a whole year.

Dear Jordan,

I just turned 16 today. I want you to know I am doing well and am healthy and happy. Things have worked out for me this last year, and I hope they have for you, too. Remember, I told you the money was going to save my life? Getting out of the city has given me a whole new way of living, and I'm independent and free. I cannot thank you enough and hope you always look back upon the help you gave to a desperate friend and know just how wonderful you are.

Enclosed is your $60, plus $20 interest. I am also sending you a little painting of the pond near my house. When you look at it, think good thoughts of me. Good luck in college.

Your grateful friend, Jenna

I put one of my small canvases, the letter, and the bills in a plastic bag. Tomorrow, I'll put on my head net and deliver it to the cache. I'm getting squared up with the world! Bet he will sure be glad to get his money back and hear I am all right. I didn't know if I could do it a year ago, but I have made it this far.

In my latest string of self-portraits, a pretty good likeness is beginning to emerge. It's hard work to get it right, and even though my book tells me there is a golden mean—basic proportions you can count on in the human face—everyone is so very different. I've spent a couple of weeks working in front of my little mirror, studying and sketching my nose, the set and shape of my eyes, the shape of my forehead, how my neck hooks into my head and how my features wrap around that sphere that is my skull. I'm trying to work out some of the colors in my skin, hair and eyes, too. It's a weird experience to study myself for so long. It's like looking into Henry's pond—shows the depth of my soul—and often the depth of my frustration when the first attempts turned out looking so goofy. I've used up a whole Pinky eraser!

Skip is by to visit and I ask him if it is okay to sketch him while we talk. He thinks it is pretty funny at first and poses like Napoleon with his hand tucked in his fishing vest, but after a while he relaxes and we go back to a comfortable silence while his pipe smoke wreathes around his head, and he kicks back around the campfire. I try to draw his high forehead with receding hairline, his straight nose, his thick moustache that droops over his upper lip, completely hiding it from view. In the winter, he grows a beard, but in the summer he shaves it off, revealing a square chin. His eyes are deep set and dark brown and his brows black and bushy. A raised, white scar runs down through his right eyebrow, bisects his eye socket and ends in a jagged line down on his cheekbone. Drawing this scar feels intimate, painful, and my pencil moves unsurely—but this is Skip. He is not Skip without this scar, even though I wish with all my heart it wasn't there. His hair is straight, self-cut, and shaggy in back, the sides partially covering big ears set closely to his head. Sometimes he wears it in a man bun, but not today. Some gray hairs are creeping in around his temples. His is a strong face, not groomed enough to put on a suit and tie and get away with it in the city, but a trip to the barber and a good clothing store, and you would know you are looking at a man with character, honesty, and a will to survive. Totally, awesomely sisu.

He's really interested in the solar lantern Carol has given to me. He fusses with it, turning it around and around in his hands as I sketch, pushing all the buttons, and this afternoon I can tell it's all he can do to keep from taking it apart to see how it works.

"Skip, man, leave that alone. I need that thing."

"Okay, okay. Just lookin' at it. Pretty neat, eh? Where do you s'pose she got this? Would be great for followin' my trap line in the winter. The days are so short, dontcha know, and I hate wastin' money on batteries."

"She said something about the boat rental place in Birch Bay, but I dunno for sure. It is great to read by instead of listening to and smelling a kerosene lamp." I make a mental note to ask Carol to buy one for him.

"Skip, tell me about trapping animals for fur. I love my fox hat, but I keep thinking about that fox, for some reason."

He put the solar lamp down and stared into the fire. "My interest in fur trappin' began when I was a young kid. Mom and Dad didn't have extra money to buy me things from the store, and, sometimes when the weather didn't let Dad work in the woods after Mom died, I had to help pitch in to pay the bills. The house I grew up in was in the woods but had power runnin' to it, a phone line, and a road to town for me to catch the bus to school. Dad had a Dodge Power Wagon and kept my mom's old Chevy for me to drive. Dad and I grew apart and were sort of livin' our own lives by the time I hit high school, but we generally got along.

"If I wanted to play football or other sports, I had to pay the fees myself. If I took the Chevy to drive into Birch Bay to take your mom on a date, I had to pay for the gas. Back in the day, us boys were expected to foot the whole bill when we took a girl out. We liked to get someone's neighbor to buy us some beer in the early spring. We'd all go out in our cars and trucks to a thick grove of white birch trees and swing on 'em."

"What? Swing on 'em?"

"Yeah. It was fun. All the boys and some of the girls tried it. Your mom was pretty good at it. We would drive our cars out at night and turn our headlights onto the grove so we could sorta see. We would find a pretty stout birch tree and one of the heavier boys would climb up it as far as he could until the trunk would begin to bend. He would ride it down toward the ground until a couple of other fellows could grab the top branches. Then a smaller guy or a girl would grab hold up at the top of the trunk and the boys would let go. The idea was to go on a wild ride through the air, branches slappin' you all the way. If you were good at it, you could ride the tree trunk up to the highest point and use the momentum to launch you on to another tree and ride it down. It was good to have had a beer or two before you tried it, 'cause it was fun but risky. There is nothing like the combo of beer and hormones to make a teenager feel invincible. Our buddy Charlie broke an arm one night when he lost his grip and flew off into a pine tree by accident. We dumped him off at Doc's house and burned rubber to get away before he reported our drunkenness to all our dads. Of course, they found out soon enough, and we had to face the music. I used to like to climb up solo until the tree started to bend and then transfer to the next tree and so on and so forth, kinda like a monkey. When we would head for home, those poor trees were pretty beat down in our rear view mirrors. I don't think they ever really recovered, but we had our fun.

"Well, I got distracted tellin' you about a cheap date in the UP. HA! You asked about trappin'.

"Trappin' was somethin' I could do to make some pretty good money on the weekends. Most of my friends and their dads trapped, too. Some girls even took it up. I would set the traps on Friday after school, pick them up on Saturday evening, and skin and stretch the pelts of anything I was lucky enough to catch on Sunday after Dad and I got back from church and had our dinner. At the end of the month, I would roll up the pelts and take them to the fur buyer, who came by Birch Bay. The cash would come home. I would settle anythin' I owed Dad, make a contribution to the bills if we needed it that month for food, put gas in the car, and spend the rest on myself. I tried to put some aside for that ring for your mom, too, when I got into high school and knew she was for me. Still got that ring in my dresser drawer. When I run into it searchin' for clean socks, I can finally look at it without gettin' in the dumps."

He is getting sad, so I ask another question, "I liked the way you killed the doe with one shot, but doesn't trapping hurt the animals?"

"Yes, it does sometimes. I won't deny that, but if you know what you are doin' and take a little care, you can make sure the animals don't suffer long. There's some kinds of traps and techniques I don't use because I don't like to cause an animal undue pain, but I couldn't live so independently off the land without killin' animals and gettin' income from my furs, food from the venison, fish, and my chickens. I'm able with my trappin' and small military disability payments to put aside enough cash to pay my property taxes each year and buy the things I can't get from the land. I follow all the rules set by the DNR, and the population of animals is healthier than ever. Everybody out here livin' in the bush don't always do everythin' legal-like, but I've always respected the law, and when Victor, the game warden, stops by my cabin for coffee and a visit, I never have anythin' to hide.

"Now, let me see that picture you are drawin' of me, eh." I hand the sketchpad to him. "Hmmm. I like this sketch up here in the corner. Always knew I looked a bit like Leonardo."

"DaVinci?"

"Heck, no! DiCaprio! That was the last movie I ever saw. The sinkin' of the Titanic—or somethin' like that, eh. Never forget watchin' him drown in all that ice water. Took me two days to warm up!"

Next thing I knew, he was out the door, his big laugh echoing across the pond. A big blue heron spread his huge wings and rose up protesting at his approach through the ferns. Crrrrakkk! Crrrakk! *Swish, thump, swish, thump.*

Chapter 31

"So you know your neighbor, Skip, huh?" Carol pulls his portrait from the pile of drawings on her lap. I had left her a note to meet me at the cache, and it is great to see her.

"Well, yeah, I do." How much to tell? *Trust, Jenna, trust.* Uncle Bill's voice in my head again.

"Good. I was hoping you two neighbors had found each other. Fine man, Skip. He's got sisu, like you." I had to smile.

"He and I got off to a rocky start, but he's my best friend, and has helped me out a million times. Speaking of helping me out, here is a letter and my money for my friend Jordan."

"OK. I'll get this turned into a money order and send it to him. He only has my phone number, not my address. Do you want to hear back from him, or should I leave my return address off?"

"Just leave it off for now, please. That life is behind me. Seems like I've been here forever—but in a good way," I add.

"Okay, I'm sure you will tell me about your situation someday, if you want to, but today is what we have before us—not yesterday—or tomorrow, and we must make the best of it. A very wise woman Pema Chodron tells us: 'The source of wisdom is whatever is going to happen to us today. The source of wisdom is whatever is happening to us right at this very instant.' In fact, I want to grab this moment. Come with me. Bring your sketchpad."

She firmly grasps my hand and hauls me to my feet. This woman is so strong. My drawings go gently into the cache, my sketchpad into the deerskin backpack Skip helped me make, and off we go on the rough trail to the right. I have watched her head in this direction before. Seems like we are heading right into the middle of nowhere.

We walk at least an hour through thick pines and navigate carefully through an ugly clear-cut full of downed branches, thick berry brambles, and randomly spaced tree stumps: every tree harvested to make paper. We have to balance carefully to traverse a slippery log over a roiling stream. Suddenly, there is the sweet perfume of woodsmoke in the air. The fragrance is so unexpected it stops me in my tracks. Hope we aren't walking into a forest fire.

"Wait here." She holds her palms up and I obey.

She is gone for what seems to be forever, but then I hear her call and move toward her voice. I step into a small meadow and am greeted by a forest scene that is so beautiful it is unreal. A gnarly-looking mutt of a dog runs out to greet me, head up, tail wagging, bouncing on his front legs in a playful hello. In the middle of the meadow is a short, circular, domed structure, a little taller than me and maybe twelve feet across. The outside is covered with large white slabs of birch bark layered over each other and lashed together by four vertical rings fashioned from small, flexible birch trunks. It reminds me of an igloo. A thick animal hide covers the doorway. Lichens, mosses and ferns line the path, and smoke curls from the short chimney of an outdoor oven. I smell yeast bread baking for the first time since I walked past the bakery in Chicago on the way to school. My stomach growls in response. The scene is one right out of my American history book from back in the day.

Carol is standing beside a dark-haired woman in a long dress. The small woman is sitting on a wooden bench with a light plaid blanket around her shoulders. She seems very, very old to me, however my ideas of age have changed since knowing Carol. Her dark face is lined, weathered. Her complexion a contrast to the lily-white Carol by her side.

"Jenna, I would like you to meet Megis. She and her ancestors have been in this area since 3,000 years before Christ, if you can wrap your mind around that! I'm glad to have two of my friends together." Megis welcomes me with a warm smile and a wave of her hand. As I come near, I see Carol holding something, turning it all about and admiring it.

"Jenna, look at this exquisite work." She passes a small, circular, lidded box to me. The surface colors glow with a beautiful matte finish, and it is made of a sturdy, hard material I have never seen before. Light as a feather.

"This is so cool. What's it made of?"

Megis answers in a soft, patient voice. "I have fashioned this box from birch bark and decorated it with dyed porcupine quills. Sit down here and I will show you the technique I use." I sit on the bench next to her. A smudge of flour from bread-baking is on her forehead. She smells of herbs and wood smoke. In the expanse of the lap of her skirt are all her materials: pliers, a handmade tool to poke holes, and different lengths of what I now recognize to be trimmed porcupine quills…some dyed red, blue, and different shades of brown.

She takes up a circular piece of white birch bark that has the beginning of a wonderful star design. With steady hands, she first pokes several holes in the bark. It's not easy to push the tool through the tough bark, but takes patience and strength. When she is happy with the holes, she chooses a quill of the correct length and color and inserts each end into the holes. The pliers are used to pull the quill tightly into the design so it is seated firmly next to the others with no bark showing between.

"These quills are dampened so they are somewhat flexible now. When they dry they will be hard, and I can trim them. The Creator fashioned quills out of stuff like your fingernails. Once I get all the parts of the box decorated, I will assemble it with grass lashings."

"I've got a question, Megis. How do you get quills off a porcupine? Surely you can't just go up to one and ask for them." We all laugh at that one.

"No, the porcupine has to give his life one way or another. All the quills I could ever want are brought to me. One of the local trappers catches one by accident every once in a while and brings it to me.

Our friend, Carol here, comes with quills from ones she finds killed on the road."

"Yuck, Carol!"

"Well, I don't carry the bloody mess out here, Jenna. I keep a wool blanket in my trunk in a plastic bag. The locals know when I come to a screeching halt and jump out of my Subaru there's a squashed porkie. They don't bat an eye when they see me rolling a smelly carcass around in the blanket by the side of the road. That technique pulls off a bunch of quills Megis can use. I fold up the blanket, toss it in the plastic bag, stow it in my car, and carry out here." As if to take the attention off her reckless driving, she says, "Look at the bottom of this box, Jenna. A small yellow star is centered there. That is her signature. Megis means star. Isn't that neat?"

"Sure is. Would you be willing to teach me how to do this, Megis?"

"I would be willing to teach, but I won't teach YOU." She looks me right in the eyes when she says this, and the insult stings. Confused, I look at Carol. She seems as surprised at Megis's statement as I am. I feel like standing up and walking away from this woman. Her words are selfish and mean. Who does she think she is anyway?

She senses my anger and confusion, turns toward me, and puts a warm hand on my wrist, keeping me at her side. Her voice is gentle once again. "Let me try to explain. Quillwork is an ancient craft of the Anishinaabe. The symbols I work into my boxes give the object a living spirit and usefulness. It is not just a pretty thing to put on a shelf to collect dust. In my work, I am sharing a small expression of our culture, which, like our native language, has struggled to survive. I would like to teach this skill to young women and men of my tribe, not outsiders like you, who cannot claim the same spiritual connection or give these objects true life.

"My strong words to you come from frustration that the young people of the tribe are so busy making their way in the outside world they think the old ways hold them back and keep them from making big salaries, and, unfortunately, they are right. For me, I have to do what is in my heart. I am most at peace in the woods. I am blessed to have time to think, pray, create and be whole.

I am beginning to understand. "Megis, do you live here alone all year around?"

"I have a daughter in Negaunee. My little dog and I spend the bitter winter months with her, but I always look forward to coming back to my camp in the spring. I do not live in the future. I honor the past and live as fully in the present as I can. That means I have to do it alone—but not lonely. The living things that surround me are my company and comfort."

Her words ring true to all I have learned in the past two years, and I find myself going from anger and insult to great respect for this woman by my side. I have to wipe away a tear. I nod and finally look her in the eyes. Our hearts connect. She looks over at

Carol, who has stayed silent while we make our peace. She speaks with love in her voice.

"Our friend Carol is a lifeline for me and others. She respects my choices and helps me find purpose and an outlet for my talents. It was a great day when she stumbled into the clearing soaking wet and shivering from an unexpected rain. She became my overnight guest, and we laughed and sang until dawn. And that was that." The two women beam at each other.

Carol sits down on one of Megis's two outdoor chairs to have a visit, and I retreat to do some sketching with her permission…her house, her friendly dog, the clearing, fish fillets drying on a rack, the outdoor oven and fragrant, cooling loaves. She doesn't care for me to do a close-up portrait, but it is okay for me to draw her in her environment, so I sketch impressions and make a note of colors I would use in a final pastel or painting. I pull a corner of the animal hide at her door and peek inside. Maybe if we come back again she will show me the inside of her little shelter. I catch a quick glimpse of colorful blankets on a cot.

The two women chat and laugh and finally Carol stands and they hug. Carol carefully wraps one of the finished boxes and places it in her pack. She give Megis an envelope and a small gift box of chocolates. Cash, I assume, from the sale of her beautiful crafts and candy as a special treat.

We hike back to my cache in relative silence. I automatically reach out to steady Carol on the stream crossing. After all, she is carrying precious cargo in that pack. I am in sort of a fog, processing all I have seen and heard, and can't wait to get back to Loon Haven, grab a snack to satisfy my growling stomach, and get to work putting some of my sketches on larger paper. I never dreamed there were people and places like this. Different drummers, indeed.

Chapter 32

I awake from a vivid dream again and am disoriented. I have fallen asleep on the cot in the cabin instead of in my tent. My latest canvas stands on a makeshift easel Skip and I have fashioned from birch limbs. As I regain my senses, I remember working very long into the night on my latest attempt to capture Megis baking bread in her oven. The whole scene is washed in the soft colors of early morning. The coals in her oven are banked, glowing in readiness, and she is using a wooden peel to load the oven and to move the loaves around to bake evenly. I am hoping to summon up the fragrance of bread baking in my viewer's mind, and I feel that I am on the right track. Some subtle shading suggests the movement of a gentle morning breeze wafting the smoke and the yeasty aroma in soft swirls across the canvas.

I'm still groggy and there is a good chance I will be able to fall back asleep in my tent for a couple more hours. I stagger toward the porch but am met by a musical greeting coming from the direction of the two-track to the cabin. Geez! What's got her up so early this morning, and what's she doing here? I rub my sleepy eyes and straighten my twisted clothing I have slept in all night. There's no point trying to hide from her.

"May I come on?"

I sighed. No more sleep for me. "Yeah, sure. C'mon in. I'll make coffee."

"Oh, good! I've had one cup but could use another." She sweeps into the cabin—a ball of fire already today. She gives me a quick hug, smiles at my disheveled appearance, and immediately parks herself, hands on hips, in front of my canvas. She studies it carefully and without comment while I build a small fire with kindling to get the coffee going. She is quiet for so long, I figure something must be really wrong with my painting. Why do I second guess myself all the time? If I'm going to make art my life, I have to be able to take criticism. Just the other day, I copied one of Henry's long quotes and pinned it near the stove. I read it again, now. *…if one advances confidently in the direction of his dreams, and endeavors to live the life which he has imagined, he will meet with a success unexpected in common hours. If you have built castles in the air, your work need not be lost; that is where they should be. Now put the foundations under them.*

Yes. These words are Uncle Bill, Henry, Skip, Grandma, Grandpa, Carol, Megis, and Mom all speaking to me. They are my posse, my team. I have passed that invisible boundary, built castles both here on the ground—I smile as I think of the castle I am standing in—and also in the air and am now putting the foundations under them. I know how important foundations are; a good one protected me from a hungry bear and gave me power I had never known before! *You've got sisu, kid!*

I carry over a steaming cup of black coffee, her preference, and stand shoulder to shoulder with Carol as she continues to gaze at my latest work. She finally speaks.

"I am beginning to see a style emerge in your work, Jenna. As you've learned to observe the natural world, you've tuned in to the organic shapes and the ways color and light and shadow interact. In this painting, I can smell bread baking on the wisps of air." I smile, but keep quiet. "The forest is rendered beautifully in the early morning sun and lifting fog. You seem less skilled at placing the human elements in nature, but I think that's because you lack experience in human observation. Megis would say she recognizes the spirit of each tree and lichen in this scene, but that she and her home are not painted with that same power and respect."

I can immediately see what she is talking about. It is true. Megis looks pasted onto a beautiful forest scene. Unnatural.

"Hmmm. I see that. Of all the possible humans to be living in this scene, she certainly deserves to blend in. Look. I have given her little dog more spirit than I show in Megis. Wonder what is going on in my head?"

"I think it's both technical and, as you say, in your head. You have had over a year studying the forms of nature. You have only spent a short time looking at the human face and form, so your technique is not as advanced. It would definitely be tricky to make Megis and her surroundings blend and flow with the forest the way they do when you walk into her clearing as into a fairy tale. I couldn't do it.

Piano playing is my game, but I can see your glaring errors here. In your mind, perhaps Megis doesn't really belong in the scene, taking up space in the forest. Maybe you are carrying some prejudice toward people, especially those who are different from you."

I began to object. "Are you saying I'm a racist?"

"No, I am saying it takes maturity to finally realize the worth of every living thing and to see how each fits into the scheme of life. It's hard to have trust and respect for one, if you don't have it for all. I've discovered that in my long life, and it has been a challenge to practice it, especially when I know I am supposed to love the unloveable. Maybe you are just a tad jealous another woman has made a success of a self-reliant life for many years. The life you have made for yourself out here is an accomplishment, but you are far from unique, as I hope you will see again this morning. I've given you a lot to think about. Let all this simmer in your young brain and let's go! A third cup of coffee can wait."

"Let's go? Where the heck are we going now?"

"Me to know and you to find out."

"Oh, man. Here we go again." I pulled a sweatshirt off the peg.

"Put on your boots. I feel a hike coming."

We head up the two-track toward the road. I haven't walked this direction since my arrival at the cabin. "Why are we headed this way, fearless leader?"

"Ha. I'm taking you on a ride. Surprise!"

My stomach tightens up. "You know I don't like to be around a bunch of people, right?"

"We won't be, but where we are going is too far to walk from your place."

A little green car is sitting by the side of the two-track. "I didn't figure you wanted anyone to drive up to the house. You have told me about that gun!" She grins. "Plus, the overgrown bushes might scratch my delicate finish." She smiles at her dingy car, with dented front fender and faded top.

She tosses a couple of hats and a Kleenex box from the passenger seat to the back and motions me into the car. I haven't ridden in a car for forever, but at least this time I'm not driving! She starts the car with a roar, backs out, throwing me forward against the seat belt, and then spins gravel as she tears down the dirt road. The radio is blaring: classical music with an irritating undercurrent of static. She turns the radio down and fusses with the fan control as we fly along kicking up dust in our wake. I'm reminded of Ratty taking that wild ride with Mr. Toad in a book our teacher read to us back in the day. I wish she would just keep two hands on the wheel. This isn't the way I had envisioned dying: strapped next to a preacher woman on a mission.

After three sharp turns onto smaller and even smaller two-track roads, Carol pulls off the road into the weeds and hits three sharp blasts on her wimpy little horn: *poot, poot, poot.* She grabs two shopping bags from the back and hands the heavier looking one to me. I glance inside: a tin of pipe tobacco, a big bottle of Canadian whiskey, sugar, salt, coffee, and toilet paper. What a grocery list! We head onto an indistinct trail into the forest, climb up a rise, and walk for half an hour or so before I smell the familiar woodsmoke greeting us.

I am again transported to a scene from long ago. A small, tidy cabin built from gray, precisely squared-off timbers is situated in the middle of a clearing. A wisp of smoke drifts from a stone chimney. The covered porch has two handmade chairs and a small table. I recognize an outhouse set back behind a woodpile that looks like a piece of art—each stick straight, small, and stacked to dry in chimney fashion. Carol points out the smoke house for curing and storing venison and fish and the sauna: the traditional Finnish way to keep clean. Skip has told me no house up north is complete without a "sow-nah", and that's how to pronounce it so you don't sound ignorant up here. A lazy mutt of a dog raises his head to check us out and then goes back to snoozing by his doghouse.

Carol calls out a high, musical, "Woo hoo! Woo hoo!"

Onto the porch strolls a white-haired old man, dressed in a pressed black suit, white shirt, and narrow tie. He is clean-shaven and bright-eyed. His back is straight. He is trim and fit. He bounces down the steps and advances on us with a big smile.

"Carol!"

"Kaarlo! How good to see you."

He takes Carol's shoulders firmly in hand, leans down, and plants a big long kiss right on her mouth! I didn't think preachers kissed on the lips, especially old preachers. Then he advances on me. I take a couple of steps back, but he is not discouraged.

"Who is this beautiful gal, eh?" His strong fingers grip my shoulders and he plants a long kiss square on my mouth, too! OMG! This is my first real kiss and it comes from an ancient person! I am tempted to turn around and flee back to the car, but then he holds me out at arm's length and looks at me with piercing blue eyes, the color of a clear summer sky. He's evaluating me, and I'm getting pretty uncomfortable here. I glance at Carol and she is puttering around with the grocery bags, abandoning me. I figure I can outrun everyone I've met so far up north, except for that bear—and maybe this frisky, old man.

"So, who are you missy, eh?"

"What do you mean, sir?" I figure I better be polite here.

"What's da name?"

"Jenna....Jenna Burke."

"Burke? Dat's not from round here. Are you's a troll?"

I knew a troll was a way for a Yooper to describe a downstater who lived below the bridge, the Mackinac Bridge, that is. It was not a compliment.

"No. I live up here—have for a while now—and my family owns a cabin. My mother's name was Lehto, Alissa Lehto."

"Oh, Lehto, eh. Well, you's is okay, den." A big grin created wrinkles all over his face, his blue eyes flashed.

Carol overhears our conversation and laughs. "You passed the test, Jenna. Got enough Finn in you to belong in the northwoods, according to Kaarlo's standards. I could never pass the test, but he puts up with me, right, Kaarlo?"

"You's is okay, Carol. Got sisu."

"Back atcha, my friend."

While I have been getting the third degree, Carol has set the porch table with a tray and three etched crystal glasses. I take a seat on the top step while my elders settle into the two comfy-looking rockers. Two chairs for company, three for a crowd, like Henry says. Guess I qualify as the crowd. Kaarlo cracks open the bottle of whiskey and pours each of us a very small measure.

"Kinda early in the day for drinkin', but here's to Missy. Kippis, ladies." The crystal rings out as we gently tap our glasses, repeat "Kippis," and take a sip. Another first—never tasted whiskey before. Whew! It's warm, strong, and burns a little going down. I politely set down my glass, as Kaarlo pours another round for the two of them.

Kaarlo encourages me to poke around his house and buildings, while he and Carol have a visit. His front door, divided in two halves top and bottom, is standing open, so I wander into the small house. Everything has a special place in this one room, and it is cozy and neat as a pin. Three colorful china plates of various sizes are organized in a wall rack hanging over a small butcher-block kitchen counter. There is a metal dishpan on the counter to serve as a sink, knives protrude from slots in the counter. A brightly colored dishtowel, white with big red flowers, hangs on a wooden rod. A small, ornate cast iron woodstove with a moose and pine tree design stands in the middle of the cabin, a shiny copper teakettle on top.

A black stovepipe extends up to a metal box and through the roof. A small cot, made up neatly with cotton sheets, a brightly quilted coverlet, and an orange and blue patterned pillow, takes up one corner of the cabin. These colors against the blonde interior timber walls are rich and magnificent. I try to store them in my memory to paint later. A round handmade table is next to the bed and holds a Bible and a small kerosene lamp. Shelves pegged into the walls in strategic places hold a collection of smoking pipes, some fishing gear, and a deer rifle. Another graceful rocking chair is under the front window. A footstool is covered with yet another colorful patterned tapestry. His working clothes both hang on pegs and are folded onto the shelves above them. I realize he used the few minutes after Carol's honking to change into what must be his best suit.

Peeking into the dark smokehouse, I am met by a salty sweet fragrance that makes my mouth water. I can hear the two of them still laughing and chatting, so I sit down and make a few sketches—even one of his sleeping dog. I note the colors I see and the bright shafts of sunlight coming down onto the clearing. I wonder how I can capture that.

Wandering onto the back porch of the cabin, I find Kaarlo's workshop. He makes beautiful wooden water buckets and ladles like the one on the ground outside his sauna. I run my hands over his wood supply, his tool handles, and pick up and study one of the finished products on the shelf—gorgeous and useful, too.

Before long, Carol calls my name. I walk around the cabin to find Carol and Kaarlo in a clinch. Of course, he embraces me, as well. I have to admit, he is a good hugger. If this guy were only 21, I think I could enjoy looking into those blue eyes every day of my life. *Jenna, you're getting weird here. Been in the woods too long.* Carol picks up one of the grocery totes and hands me one of Kaarlo's beautiful buckets and a ladle to carry back to the car. "Hei, Hei!" He calls out to us with a wave. "Bye, bye," Carol responds.

Back at the car, I peek in the grocery tote to find a small box full of buttons fashioned from wood and bone. "Those are antler bone buttons, Jenna. Between selling these sauna buckets, dried mushrooms, smoked fish, buttons, and backpacks of woven birch bark, Kaarlo keeps busy and gets along pretty well. He has a daughter who also comes in the summer for a week to make sure he is okay. He treats her like a queen and she honors him. They spend one day in Marquette buying clothes to get him through the winter, and she walks through the sporting goods store with him to choose a Christmas present. She has tried to get him to leave the woods and to come to live in her warm, beautiful home in the horse country of Kentucky, but he won't budge. They don't fight about it, though. She knows when she is licked, and I don't think I have ever witnessed such a deep connection between father and child. If we all could accept and respect each other's choices, what a world we would have!"

The whole way back to my cabin I don't even consider how fast we are zipping along in the little green car, and our return trip barely registers even when I realize I have been talked into helping to roll a smelly, dead porcupine in a wool blanket. My mind's eye is focused on how I will improve my Megis painting and also capture Kaarlo's sun-dappled clearing.

Chapter 33

"Hello in the house!"

"Skippy! Haven't seen you in like forever." I rise up from organizing my jumble of wood. Inspired by Kaarlo, I'm trying to turn my beaver dam woodpile into a work of art.

"Yeah, wait 'til I tell you my adventure, Jenna."

"Great. I'll put on a pot of coffee."

Mugs in hand, we settle on the porch steps, his bad leg outstretched. He lights his pipe.

"So, spill it."

"Well, there's a guy back in the deep woods who I've run across on my trapline from time to time. Won't tell anyone his name. Hidin' from the law or family—or just has his own reasons for livin' like he does, and that's okay by me. I stumbled into his camp by mistake once, and his three big wolf-dogs nearly scared me up a tree, bad foot and all. He called them off just as I was tryin' to scramble up a pine. Had a 12 gauge with him, not exactly trained on me, but unsettlin', anyway. I introduced myself and told him I meant no harm and would be on my way, but he simmered down and said if I didn't mind he could use a hand with something. Curiosity got the better of me, and he was still holdin' that gun, so I said okay. He led me back to one of those sod houses like you see in pictures of the pioneers on the prairie. It was mostly a dugout in the ground, not more than twelve by twenty feet, covered by a thick layer of soil and grown all over by ferns—no way you could see it from the air—could walk right by it and not recognize it as a shelter. Put me in mind of a bear cave.

Some of the roof had collapsed. I helped him lift a couple of timbers to repair it. We lugged them over and set them in place, and he forced out a few words of thanks. I could tell he was really out of the habit of talkin' to a human, probably only interactin' with his dogs, and most of that in Finnish. I think he takes them into his dugout to keep him warm at night like the people do up north because I didn't see any stovepipe anywhere. You've heard of a three dog night—that's a cold one. He must cook his meals on a campfire. Probably survives on pemmican in the winter, which is dried fish, blueberries, and duck fat all mashed together and wrapped tightly in a deer intestine, like a salami. It is full of protein and stores forever. He smirks, "Betcha end up with powerful breath."

"Ewww, Skip."

"I know. Sounds tasty, eh?"

"I admired the beautiful Finnish axe he was usin'. Wide blade and beautiful wooden handle. He had cut those timbers so true with it. My compliments seemed to please him, and he led me into the woods to see his forge set-up. Right there in the woods, he was making these steel axes with wooden handles. It's gettin' to be a lost art of those old-time Finnish blacksmiths. Those things are worth $200 or more for the ones industrial-made in Finland, not even hand forged. His blade was so sharp it could split a whisker.

"I come to find out he has a cache like yours, but Carol has only seen him once when she stumbled across him like I did and ended up halfway up a tree. He and his dogs snarled at her in no uncertain terms to get out and not come back, and she respected that, but, you know her and her collection of backwoods friends; she charmed him into the cache system. She delivers borax and a few chunks of low carbon steel and hardened steel, which are the raw materials he needs in order to create two axe heads each month. The other months, she brings mineral oil, a chunk of beeswax, coffee, sugar, and matches. A bottle of good whiskey in the fall. He leaves an axe or hatchet in a leather sheath for sale and some smoked fish for her. Carol knows a man who will buy all the axes she can get. She tried to leave Axe Guy cash once, but he put it back in the cache, so she just runs a tab. So far, he's way ahead.

"Well, you coulda knocked me over with a feather, when he showed up last week on MY doorstep, those wild dogs pantin' and chargin' round sendin' my chickens squawkin' into the trees. Pulled the tail feathers out of one of the girls. I could tell the old gent was in pain, and he wordlessly pulled up his sleeve and showed me his left forearm, which was badly blistered and burned. He was finally able to make me understand one of the dogs tipped his portable forge as he was hammerin' on the anvil. He couldn't jump out of the way fast enough. He had used goose grease on his arm but had been gettin' feverish at night and knew he was in trouble.

"I know a fellow from Big Birch Lake who is a retired doc. I do some fishin' guide work for him and his friends once in a while. I got Axe Guy settled down in my house and his dogs fed, watered, and shut up securely in my woodshed, walked into town, explained the situation to Doc, and brought him back out with me. I took a roundabout way so we didn't go by your place, here. You already have a preacher in your business, figured you didn't need a doctor, too.

"Reason I haven't come to see you is because Axe Guy—he still won't tell me his name and so I have got to callin' him Buddy, has been sleepin' in my bed for a week! Took that long to get the fever and infection under control and to be able to finally send him and his dogs packin'. While he was there, I worked a little on his hygiene. Whew, guess the dogs don't care. The whole family of four smelled like a herd of wet buffalo. Buddy couldn't wait to get back to his little hidey hole. The dogs whined all night because I wouldn't let them in the house to sleep with him. I'm exhausted! Been airin' out my mattress for three days."

"Skippy, you're a heck of a guy. You've got sisu to spare. Sorry I don't have any pemmican to share with you, but Carol put some brownies in my cache—good with coffee."

"Ahh, you're a good girl, eh. I've sure missed you."

"Back atcha."

Chapter 34

The most interesting dwellings in this country, as the painter knows, are the most unpretending, humble log huts and cottages of the poor commonly; it is the life of the inhabitants…which makes them picturesque.

I'm struggling to complete a second painting of Megis, reflecting her true place in the natural environment. Carol was right. I begin with using the same free strokes I use for the sky, forest, and water and paint the birch bark shelter. When I step back to look at my progress, I'm getting there. The shelter has life and a natural place in the setting. This is exciting to begin to capture this "interesting dwelling," and the rest of the scene is falling into place. Everything, including Megis, has life and spirit in this new painting. Can't wait to see what Carol thinks.

When I turn to the sketches in my book of Kaarlo's clearing, I first determine the life of the inhabitant—Kaarlo, himself—dapper and tidy. His handcrafted dwelling reflects a passion for straight lines and square corners that contrast to the soft, curved shapes of the forest. Nature is huge and flowing around him, but his life is spent in detail, taking elements of nature and hewing and shaping them to his will: a limb or antler become buttons, round logs are squared off in precise sizes and lengths, his cabin stands fully exposed, straight and true, in a shaft of sunlight. Wood slats become watertight buckets. His life is not a blending, integrating act like Megis, but proud craftsmanship turning the raw materials of nature into items useful for himself and others. My painting must reflect this self-reliant life; he is as close to Henry in the flesh as I am going to find.

Now, Skip has given me a third setting to consider: his Buddy. I will have to paint completely from my imagination and Skip's tale, and my canvas will reflect an unnamed man's disappearing act in a location undiscovered and overlooked. A mere swelling in the earth, a bear cave with only a lingering hint of a man and his half-wild dogs.

All my efforts to envision and to paint these people and places has me wondering how I will one day paint the cabin at Loon Haven and her only human resident. Will I be a girl of four with blonde pigtails and a frog in her overall pocket, smoke rising from a campfire and uncle calling from the porch, or will I be a young woman standing in flannel by a half-demolished cabin? Who am I and how do I fit into this wild place?

The pond was here when virgin forest was home to the wolves. An Anishinaabe girl looked at her reflection in the quiet water. Loggers who took down the huge pines brushed the woodchips from their shoulders and ate their lunch of pasties and cider on the big stumps. Men searching for nickel and iron deposits walked my trails and waded the streams. The new trees grew up and the low willows and berry bushes brought in deer, moose, and bear to browse. Trees too rotten or misshapen to cut became the homes for raccoons and squirrels, and the birds nested in the second growth forest: owls, hawks, ravens, crows, chickadees, and Sisu's ancestors. Many living things have been here long before me, and many will be here after we all are gone. That's something Henry has taught me. He would also remind me I have to get ready for a second winter, so I better put down this sketchbook and get to work.

I have marked my 451st notch—64 weeks at Loon Haven. After going through one cycle of any task, I have always found the second time around to be much easier, so I make some improvements to make my wood wall a little more air tight. I borrow a mattock from Skip and widen the trail to the outhouse and put down a bark pathway to keep my pant legs dry. Carol put some waffle weave long underwear in the cache last time. It is the right size for me, but doesn't have the magical drop seat. I'll probably get the red union suit out in the coldest weather.

"Woo, hoo!" The musical call.

"Carol, what's up?"

"I see you are busy with your woodpile. Maybe you don't have time to go with me today."

"Heck, no! Are you kidding? Going with you is like a surprise trip to another place, time, and planet. Just let me put on my boots."

"Okay. My chariot awaits at the end of the lane." As we fly along yet another weirdly numbered or lettered sandy road, Carol gives me some background about the woman we are about to meet.

"Her name is Lila. She is probably in her late thirties and first came to the UP when her parents attended a gathering of the Rainbow Family of Living Light, a large group of folks from all over that gets together once a year in a national forest somewhere around the country. She was just a child on her first trip, but fell in love with the lakes and pines. She arrives with the bluebirds in the spring, pitches her tent in the same spot every year, and uses her solitary time to cut, haul, and sell pine boughs to buyers from the perfume industry. She also carves and paints beautiful wooden birds. She hitchhikes everywhere she goes. The locals are happy to pick her up because she is very pleasant company. Like the migratory birds she carves, she will pack up her camp very soon now, and head off to a warmer climate—no one knows where. She leaves absolutely no footprints behind. I want you to meet her before she goes."

Carol turns onto a paved road and accelerates to full speed. It's been a long, long time since I have moved at the highway speed limit. I feel like I need to throw out my arms and brace myself, but I resist. That is so dorky. In ten minutes, we pull over and park at a scenic pullout. Carol grabs her walking stick and backpack and heads off through the Queen Anne's lace and the ferns with me trailing behind. Another fifteen minutes finds us entering an empty clearing by a pretty little waterfall. No sign of a campsite.

"Well, shoot! She's pulled out." We settle onto the rock ledge by the waterfall and each pull an apple from Carol's pack. "Well, she'll be back like clockwork next spring, and we will pay her a visit. I want you to see her exquisite bird carvings: chickadees, juncos, jays like your Sisu, waders, and waterfowl. The legs are as delicate as matchsticks and their eyes give them life. They look as if they can hop up and take wing."

Just then, we hear a loud *caw, caw, caw*! On a dead branch in the top of a tall, straight white pine, a single crow sits, calling and calling. The echoes fill the forest.

"I think we must have just missed her. That's Poe telling her goodbye."

"Poe?"

Watch this. "Poe, c'mon, c'mon down."

The black bird lifts gracefully from the treetop and makes a wide circle before spreading its wings and landing gently on Carol's shoulder with flirt and flutter! *More! More!*

"OMG, it's talking!"

Carol laughs as Poe playfully pulls her gray curls. "Lila tried to teach him 'Evermore', but it has always come out 'More'. Works in his favor for getting snacks." Carol shares a chunk of her apple with him. He bows up and down, hops to the ground, sets the apple between his feet and begins to tear it apart and to swallow big pieces.

More! More!

"Well, you little stinker. Here's one more piece. Sorry you have lost your friend, but you know she will be back."

"Do you think Poe remembers Lila? Will Sisu remember me?"

"He doesn't just remember her; his mother and grandmother were friends of Lila's before him. Crows teach their young whom they can trust, and whom to fear. Poe will fly to me because Lila has introduced us many times and he knows my face." She gestures to the edge of the stream. "Look at the little pile of shiny rocks, clam shells, and crawdad claws on that stump. Poe often brings Lila gifts and he places them there for her."

"That's so cool! Sisu comes by every day to visit and get a snack. I never thought she might miss me when I'm not home."

We left Poe watching his lonely vigil in the treetop—inspiration for a painting of an empty void where a woman has come, made connections, and has had the courage to go, leaving no trace except for a heartbroken friend waiting patiently and faithfully for her return.

Chapter 35

Every man looks at his woodpile with a sort of affection. Henry, it's not just men who make woodpiles, dontcha know!

Snow has arrived with a vengeance this year. It is piled up to my windowsills outside, and we have had weeks of dark skies and shortening days. A couple of days ago, Skip spent the day with me by the fire. It's a couple of weeks until Christmas, but I gave him a small pastel still life of Kaarlo's sauna bucket and ladle for a holiday present. I framed it in a birch bark frame. He really liked it. He gave me a pocket knife with three blades that was a present from Uncle Bill to him back when they were teenagers. Brought tears to our eyes. I have wrapped a Monet-like painting of water lilies for Carol, whenever I see her next. Sisu was happy to get a snack ball made from cornbread crumbs and bacon grease packed together and hung where a bear can't get to it. Mr. Bear is deep into winter sleep by now, anyways.

I'm surprised to hear the crunch of snow and "Jingle Bells" in that familiar, musical voice.

"Carol! Get in here out of the cold! I can't believe your car made it up the road today!"

"Oh, my magical sleigh is at my command, Jenna! You should know that by now."

She sheds layers and layers of clothes that steam in the heat of the woodstove. "Boy, it's toasty in here. Wanted to make sure you were faring well. Looks like you have been doing lots of painting."

"Getting a lot done. Here, sit down, I want to show you the Different Drummer Series. Don't say anything until I show them all to you."

"Different drummer as in *Walden*?"

"Yes. You know that quote?"

"Sure do."

"Cool!" I point to the paintings hanging left to right on the walls. "First is my latest portrait of Skip. This one is Megis's Camp—new and improved. Next is Kaarlo's Clearing in Sunlight. Here is one I call Blacksmith's Forest Dwelling. Finally, Awaiting Her Return."

I can tell she is greatly pleased by my improving work. Her smile tells me all I need to know. I'm realistic enough to know I haven't developed all the skills I need, but I'm beginning to dream about eventually making a living doing what I love best: expressing myself with shapes, colors and imagination. A wonderful feeling of freedom warms my heart.

I present her the painting I have done for her, and she beams at me. I'm so grateful for her reaction. "I have a surprise for you, too, Jenna. Put on your warm duds and come with me."

I figure we are on our way down another snow packed road, but to my surprise we turn toward Birch Bay. I recall going this way with Uncle Bill. I'm getting anxious of her idea of a surprise. Surely, she isn't going to drag me to a Christmas party. She promised.

The road is deserted as we pass the gas station, the bar, a big, white inn, the Presbyterian Church, and turn into a driveway in front of a gaily decorated log cabin. The garage door goes up, she drives the Subaru right in, and the door rattles down behind us, settling with a thud.

"Well, honey, we're home!" She says with a laugh. "I thought since you had shown me your cabin, I would show you mine. No one else is here…and no one knows you are here with me this weekend. Thought if you were okay with it, you might like to stay until Monday in my guest quarters, but that is up to you. If you feel uncomfortable being away from home, just let me know anytime, and I will run you back out to your house. Will you promise to tell me, Jenna?"

I take a couple of deep breaths, "You've never done anything to scare or hurt me, Carol. Your surprises have always been wonderful. I'm totally out of the habit of this sort of thing, though. Yeah, I'll tell you."

"OKAY! That's swell. First, let's take a look at where you will be staying." We walk up a flight of stairs above the garage and enter a little apartment. There is a plushy-looking bed with a log cabin design on the covers and flouncy matching pillows, a desk, a sink and coffee maker, a view of Birch Bay Lake. The bathroom floor is warm and there is a tub! A bathtub!

Carol sees me drooling over that bathtub and says, "While I go in and make us an early dinner, why don't you take an hour or so to run yourself a hot bath. There are even bubbles on the shelf here, if you want them. When you are done soaking, there are PJs and a robe in the closet. I'll get my PJs on, too, and we will have our dinner down by my woodstove. You have shared your art with me, so I will play you a little after-dinner piano concert. It's a pajama party!"

I haven't been to a pajama party since I was in the third grade and took my new pink comforter to my best friend's house. I haven't thought of that in years. I can't take my eyes off that bathtub and those fluffy, white towels. Carol excuses herself and I hear her humming a Christmas tune as she descends the stairs. When this woman says she has a surprise, she's not kidding!

I haven't had a long, hot bath for years, not since the days when we could afford apartment rent, and, even then, the water never got very hot. I adjust the water until it is almost scalding and breathe in the steam. The bubbles foam up and smell like flowers. Oh, boy! The water is so hot, I have to ease myself in. It is deep enough to lean back and submerge myself to my chin. I will stay here forever and ever! Every muscle relaxes as the soft water envelops me and buoys me up. I may have even dozed a few minutes. I use a soapy washcloth to wash long, lean arms, a flat tummy, muscular legs, and maturing breasts. There is a bottle of shampoo on the tub rim, so I wash and rinse my hair, using conditioner that smells like coconut candy.

I wrap myself in a huge bath towel and find an electric hair dryer in a drawer. Electricity—gosh, almost forgot there was such a thing. It whirs and blows a hot stream of air, and I comb out the tangles and re-braid my long hair. Stepping back, I make a quick appraisal of my naked self in the huge mirror. I look way different than I remember. Stronger, fitter. An older face and an okay body. Not enough curves for a movie star—but then I wouldn't want to be one of those anyways.

In the closet, I find striped flannel pajamas along with a soft, red robe, and warm slipper socks, and so I pad my way down the stairs and toward music playing on the radio. Christmas songs. I walk through an enclosed breezeway and open the door to her house. Immediately, I smell something wonderful cooking on the stove—and yeast bread.

I wander into the house, peeking in a little bedroom and bathroom as I pass, and find Carol at the stove in the kitchen. A large Christmas tree is set up in front of massive floor to ceiling windows—all aglow. I look at it with the sort of wonder a small child has when she sees her first Christmas tree.

The dining table is set for two with ice water, cloth napkins, real silverware, and a table cloth. Red candles, surrounded by pine boughs, are in the center. I look around me and spot my water lily painting hanging in the living room in a special spot for all to see. Oh, I'm so glad!

"Beef stew and whole wheat bread tonight, Jenna. I thought you probably would like some chocolate ice cream for dessert."

"I hardly know what to say, Carol. This is all so wonderful! What a surprise! I feel like a little kid."

"At Christmastime I wish everyone could feel like a child. You deserve a little break. Everyone needs a vacation once in a while, and I wanted you to see my house. I always like to visit the houses of the people I love. Then, when I think of them, I can envision them working, at play, and at rest."

After dinner, we walk downstairs to a room with a comfortable couch and a blazing woodstove. The familiar warmth feels very good. Carol sees me standing by the woodstove with my hands outstretched.

"This house has a perfectly good gas furnace, but there is something wonderful about wood heat. I keep my wood right outside on the covered patio, so it is easy for me to manage, and in the winter, this is my favorite place to read and work. Want to hear me play?"

She sits down at the piano and I settle into the corner of the couch, pulling a coverlet over my feet. The sound of the instrument fills the room, and I watch her sitting upright on the bench, playing totally from memory, her face impassive and calm, fingers moving effortlessly over the keys. She is making something that is so difficult look so very easy. I can appreciate the years of practice it takes to perform with such skill. The same years of practice are ahead of me to master my drawing and painting, but her gentle smile assures me that there is great inner joy in creating something beautiful and being able to share it with others. Her last tune is 'Silent Night,' and she softly sings along. *Sleep in heavenly peace…sleep in heavenly peace.*

Chapter 36

I awake to the aroma of clean sheets and the warmth of a comforter covering my nose. The bed is as soft as a cloud. I don't even remember climbing the stairs to this cozy apartment, but I got here somehow. The clock says 11:30. Sun is streaming in over the carpeting. I hate to move and disturb the warm covers, so I lie still and try to regain some sense of reality.

This is Carol's world. I don't know what I imagined, but this wasn't it. To be honest, I don't think I ever wondered about Carol, thinking only of what she could do for me. Then, when she brought me to meet Megis and Kaarlo, I knew I had to share her with a small group of outsiders. Now, I am catching a glimpse of a whole other life she has here in the village. A nice home and probably a big bunch of people who depend on her.

It's noon. I'm tempted to run another bubble bath, just to warm myself to the bone again, but figure I better get up, maybe make myself useful in some way. I hang up my pajamas and discover a package of new underwear, a forest green pullover sweater, socks with a snowflake pattern on them, and two pairs of jeans on the closet shelf. I dress and take a moment to check myself out in the full length mirror. I am clean and rested, and my smile comes easier. I'm also famished.

I find a note on the kitchen counter. *Had to run out. Help yourself to anything in the fridge. Make sure to have a big glass of OJ. Don't know when I'll be back, but there is plenty of reading material, and a nice view of the lake on this sunny morning. My personal bald eagle is hunting out there. Relax. No one will bother you.*

PS I ran into Skip in the village this morning. He knows you are here for the weekend. C.

It's good Skip knows. I hadn't even considered that he would get frantic if he stopped by and didn't see evidence of me for a couple of days. *Dang, you are selfish, Jenna. Grow up.* I hear Uncle Bill chewing me out and he's right.

With that scolding fresh in mind, I wash Carol's breakfast dishes and wipe the counters. I make myself a huge ham and mustard sandwich and carry it, along with a handful of potato chips, into the living room. Pulling up a little lever gets the recliner to work, and I snuggle down to enjoy every bite of my lunch: the saltiness and snap of the chips is great. I almost forgot these awesome things exist. Carol's eagle is still swooping out over the lake that is snow-covered but drifted clean in a few shiny spots. He finally lands on the ice to snack on some little fish left behind by an ice fisherman. He's a big bird, majestic, but even his sharp talons can't keep him from slipping and sliding a bit on the crystal clear and smooth blue-gray ice. I find myself enjoying his little dance. Even the mightiest stumble once in a while and have to catch their balance. The tiny chickadees cry *deedeedee, chikadeedeedee* as they come and go with sunflower seeds from the bird feeders Carol has hung from her balcony. Little gray birds peck and hop on the patio, cleaning up the dropped seed. A bird book is on the table, and I identify these fellows easily: juncos.

After my lunch, I snoop around the house for a while, looking at all of the art on the walls and knickknacks on her shelves. I hear the garage door open and shut, and greet Carol in time to help carry in two big bags of groceries and wrapping paper.

"I'm glad you are up and around. I need help wrapping gifts for my family real fast so I can get the box to the post office today. We've only got 45 minutes until they close, so let's get crackin'!"

She points out the cupboard with the wrapping supplies and heads off to gather gifts while I put scissors, tape, ribbon, and bubble wrap on the dining room table. By the time she gets back with an armful of boxes, I have the wrapping paper all set, and we get to work. She cuts the paper to fit and wraps the box. I tape and tie with some ribbon. Carol tells me what names to put on the tags, and I try to write them in fancy script. Six gaily wrapped boxes are carefully packed into one big cardboard box in record time.

"I'll address this once I get my foot in the door at the post office. Just have to get in there before she locks the door! It's only a block away. Want to come with me?"

"Naw. I'll see you when you get back. Anything I can do besides clean up this mess?"

She glanced around. "The birdfeeders need filling. Seed's on the deck."

I step onto the deck and find a snow shovel. The sun is so nice, I don't need a coat. I take my time shoveling, tossing the snow down below. The chickadees are bold, scolding me for upsetting their peaceful lunchtime, hopping and dancing on the railing next to me. They flutter around, making me homesick for Sisu and think about Poe in his lonely vigil. One bird for each person. Here, Carol has a personal eagle and a flock. Appropriate for a preacher. I smile at the thought.

Carol is back and moving at top speed. "This is my busy season, you know. Lots of details to take care of in my profession: decorations, food, music, organizing a team to feed the homeless in Marquette, double-checking that our older and wheelchair-bound members have a way to get to services, making sure the old furnace is keeping the place warm enough and calling our resident handyman if it isn't, and picking up poinsettias from the florist in Marquette. I am lucky to have lots of people to help with details, though. Mostly, I have to coordinate, troubleshoot, write the program for the church secretary to print up, get my choir singing on key, and have meaningful sermons put together for the next three Sundays. Oh, and people designated to pass the plate! The church is almost out of debt, you know. She chuckled.

"So, with all that in mind, I'm going to abandon you to your own devices again today. Nap, scrounge a dinner, watch tv, read, and I'll see you about 9 o'clock tonight. Will you be okay?"

"Actually, that sounds amazing. I am missing my sketchpad, though. Would like to sketch so I never forget this Christmas. I noticed supplies in the cupboard. May I use them? I would love to just hang around here today."

"Help yourself to anything. Mi casa es su casa!" She turns, makes a quick trip to the bathroom, and is gone in a flash, scarf flying out behind her.

I turn, take in the whole scene, and heave a big sigh. A day all to myself in a warm, beautiful house with absolutely no chores to do. First thing first, another bubble bath, and a shower after to wash and condition my hair again! I can't wait to tell Skip about this!

I bathe, shower, dry my hair and braid it. Maybe I can ask Carol to give it a trim. It's kind of bugging me—getting too long. I dress, fix myself a salad from the fridge. Lettuce! Tomato! Carrots! Avocado! It all tastes like heaven to me. I wander down to her library, run my fingers along all the books, smile at her copy of *Walden*, and choose a beautifully bound copy of *A White Heron* by Sarah Orne Jewett. It is a lovely, small, brown and forest green book with pages that are gold at the top edge. Cool! I come back upstairs and snuggle into the recliner to read with a view of the lake.

Oh, what a story! Out of that whole library, how did I manage to find an author who knows how to speak to my heart? Young Sylvia chooses to protect a thing of natural beauty instead of destroying it to bring her family out of poverty. She goes hungry to protect something she loves with a passion way beyond her years and understanding. Tears well in my eyes, as I realize the author's true artistry—to guide her reader to connect with deep feelings in so very few pages. I realize that is what I want to achieve with my paintings. I have a lifetime to get there, and I will. Every time I pick up a paintbrush, I will think of a white heron flying free from harm.

I pull a plaid blanket up around me, recline and close my eyes for just a moment, soaking in all the comfort: the smell of the pine tree, the light of the sun streaming into the living room, the ticking of a clock on the wall. The next thing I know, I'm awakening to a growling stomach and dimming light over the lake. The last shafts of sunlight throw an orange glow over the icy surface. Magically, the Christmas tree lights spring to life automatically: jolly red, green, and blue.

Back to the fridge! I could eat a horse. Whole wheat bread, cold cuts, mayo, wiggly orange gelatin with tiny oranges stuck in it, baby carrots. I make another huge sandwich and pile my plate with chips again—can't get enough of those. I pour a Vernors ginger ale over ice—watch it fizz and sip the bright sweetness that gives me a little shiver of pleasure, a cough, and a smile. Uncle Bill always had Vernors at camp. *Made in Michigan*, he would say with pride. *Nothin' better.*

Sitting at the table, I savor every bite of my dinner and finish it off with a handful of fancy little mints from a glass dish. I wash, dry, and put away my dishes and then turn to the drawer of art supplies. Armed with a new sketchpad and good pencils, I spend several hours wandering around the house making indoor sketches: the woodstove, the library, the Christmas tree alight in front of the bank of windows, now dark. I've lost track of time but hear the garage door go up and down and get up to see if Carol needs help. She always seems to be carrying armfuls here and there, but then I hear a strange voice and so I slip into the guest bathroom.

"Thanks, Sam. I can manage my bags from here. Are you ready for tomorrow?"

"Yes, ma'am!"

The back door closes and Carol calls out, "Woo Hoo!"

"I'm here. I'll take care of the bags. You've had a long day. I'll make us some tea, okay?"

"Sounds wonderful. Thank you, dear."

Off she scurries to her bedroom. I hear water running in the shower.

Later, as we enjoy our tea, I can tell Carol has something on her mind.

"As I tell Skip, go ahead and spill it, Carol."

She laughs. "Okay. This is just a thought for you to sleep on tonight. Tomorrow is Sunday, and we will be having church."

"I think I know what you are going to say—no way. I can't get around a bunch of people who all want to know who I am and want to butt into my business. I've had a great time here, and you haven't ever pressured me. Don't start now, please. I have my reasons, Carol."

"Well, just listen a second. Here is my thought about this. I go into my office to prepare for the

10:00 service several hours early, before it is light. I thought maybe you would find it meaningful to go with me, help me get the church ready, and then you can sort of hide out in my office to listen to the service. No one would know you are there, but you would get to soak up a little Christmas spirit. It's totally up to you, and, I mean this with all my heart, don't feel one iota guilty if you aren't ready to give this a try. I just felt compelled to make the offer and let you know you would be just as safe there as you are here in my home, I promise you."

"Well, I'll think about it tonight."

"Super. That's all I ask. I'll knock on your door in the morning when I get up and see if you want to go. For now, I need to finish up a little work on my sermon and then hit the sack."

Carol smiles when she sees the Jewett book in my hand as I head off to bed, and I smile back, a little shaken by this development. Every place she has taken me physically and emotionally has helped me to grow, but this feels like dangerous territory. I still must not let down my guard.

Chapter 37

I climb out of a deep sleep to a gentle knocking on my door. It's still very dark outside. She pokes her head in the room. "Good morning, Jenna. Ready to get up, or do you want to sleep this morning?"

"I've decided to go with you, Carol, but I don't have any church clothes."

"Oh, doesn't matter. Jeans and sweaters is the usual dress code in our church. Some of the older folks still like to dress up a bit, but it isn't a rule, and, no one is going to see you anyway."

"I know, but it just feels sort of weird. I haven't been to a church service since I was a little kid. I've seen my share of church basements in the past few years, but never a service."

"Well, this will be sneaky fun! Meet me by the door in half an hour. We'll carry some stuff across the street. Lots of the congregation are lucky enough to walk to church, and I'm one of them."

Carol carries her briefcase and a poinsettia in the other arm. I have a bag of napkins and plastic silverware. We carefully pick our way across the street past snowdrifts and icy patches on the road and walk into the side door of the little white church with the steeple that looks like something straight off of a Christmas card. The inside is nothing fancy, but I follow as Carol goes around flipping on light switches and turning up the thermostat. There are some pretty stained glass windows and a wooden cross on the wall in the front of the room that has all the seats. The cross reminds me a lot of something Kaarlo would make with his Finnish tools. Simple, but classy.

We go downstairs and deliver the napkins and silverware to a tidy kitchen. Decorated tables crowd the small basement. Looks like they have little parties down here. Carol sticks her head into the room with the furnace, and we hear it roaring away. "Good," she smiles.

Her office is wood paneled and has lots of bookshelves full of churchy titles, song books, and stacks of papers. There is a small dressing room off to the side with a rack of robes and colorful scarves.

"This little room is where you will hang out when people start to arrive until the service gets underway, then you can come out and sit in this comfy chair to listen, okay? At the end of the service, you can head back into the room and eavesdrop on my conversations until I tell you it is okay to come out. This is kind of fun to have a stowaway on board at Christmas time!"

It's all going like clockwork. And, I have to admit, this is kinda fun. Carol puts on her black robe over her regular clothes and chooses a colorful scarf that hangs way down on both sides. She looks great in that robe—really professional and pretty with her curly gray hair. She gives me a big smile and scampers away, robe flying! I'm impressed. I sit on a folding chair in the little closet and listen to people arrive, greet each other, hang up their coats, and walk into the big room. They are all so friendly with one another. There is quiet laughter, a few sneezes and coughs, a rustle of paper, shuffle of boots, and squeak of the seats as everyone seems to get settled in to listen.

As soon as I hear Carol welcome everyone and call their attention, I peek outside the closet. Coast is clear. Taking the chair near her desk, I can hear everything that is going on. With the swish of her robe, I can tell she has taken her place at the piano, and the small congregation pipes up with a song with lots of verses. Then, the robe rustles again and she reads something from the Bible and says a prayer. The prayer is cool because she prays for the whole world, the countries in it, the state, the many people in it, the village of Birch Bay and everyone here, the people sitting in the room, down to those who couldn't come today for whatever reason. That was one huge prayer, for sure. It was awesome! How does she get up there and speak from her heart in front of a room full of people? I would be terrified.

She invites people to make announcements and tell news. A woman talks about how many little girl dresses and cloth diapers have been sewn by the ladies in the village and sent to Africa. Another gives the results of the profits from the Christmas craft sale. Some money will be put in the bank to help keep the lights and heat on in the church over winter. The rest is going to feed the struggling homeless population in Marquette. In a quavering voice, an old man thanks the congregation for their prayers and for helping him get to his doctor's appointments. He is feeling much better, and people actually clap for him right there in the church! I guess I'm getting in the spirit of all of this because I have to stop myself from clapping, too, and giving myself away. We find out that the family that got burned out of their house has found a place to rent with combined help from this church and the Catholic Church across the street. Someone's mother has died downstate. If you want to contribute toward flowers, put your money in an envelope behind the pew—oh, yeah, that's what those seats are called—and mark it Flowers for Jane. Upcoming events include a midnight service on Christmas Eve and morning service on Christmas Day. Party at Carol's following for everyone. Applause for that, too.

Then it is back to more serious stuff. The little choir sings, more prayers are said, and I hear the clink of collection plates being handed down the aisles. Everyone stands up to sing and sits back down to hear Carol give a little talk about the special time of year and how Jesus teaches we are to love the unlovable, even if it's really hard to do. Seems like a good thing to remind people about on Sunday, but, of course, it is easy to listen and agree when you are sitting around feeling sort of holy. The trick is if these folks will do the hard part on Monday. I hope, for Carol's sake, they will.

I hear her introducing someone to sing a solo. Oh, boy, that sounds sort of like a recipe for disaster. Her robe rustles and a familiar *Silent Night* begins followed by a wonderful voice—a man—but, wait, not so deep, and clear as a bell. *Silent night, Holy night,*

Shepherds quake at the sight. I am intrigued enough to take a little peek around the doorframe. Gosh. It's a boy! I suddenly realize I haven't seen anyone my age for eons! His dark hair is sort of long but combed neatly. He is tall, in a gray sweater and dark pants. His is no ordinary voice. He sings effortlessly, and he and Carol look at one another from time to time. When the final notes fade away, you can hear a pin drop. I discover I have been holding my breath.

We are both famished when we sneak back across the road and into the house. I smell the rich fragrance of roast chicken. Carol had put it into the oven before we left for church, and it is making my mouth water. We work side by side in the kitchen.

"Okay, tell me. Who is he?"

Carol looks at me with an impish grin. "Who, Jenna?"

"Oh, c'mon. You know who I'm talking about."

She laughs. "Oh, Sam? I've known him since I arrived here and have tried to encourage that wonderful voice of his. He's heading off to the University of Michigan to study vocal music and education. Wants to be a teacher. He plays the piano, too. He and I are wonderful friends. I like his parents a lot. There aren't many young people in this village, so Sam is eighteen going on thirty, know what I mean? You couldn't see, but he is the only young person in a sea of gray-haired folks in my congregation. The UP is getting awfully old because it is hard for a family to make a living up here, so we do our best taking care of each other as we age in place. When a family's history is in the UP, people hate to leave, even if it makes sense to get somewhere warmer. We have lots of "snowbirds": Yoopers who head to Florida for part of the winter, but they get homesick, and we welcome them back by Easter. The two village churches are lifelines for their members and love for our neighbors spills out onto those who don't want to have anything to do with church, as well. Do what is right and good, no matter if you follow a religious creed or not. What a wonderful world, if we would only just do it. Well, you already heard me preach once. You don't need another sermon! Let's eat!"

After lunch, Carol disappears into her home office to make phone calls, and I am enjoying another afternoon of reading in this glorious recliner chair. If I had one of these in my cabin, I would have to pry myself out of it to get anything done. We share an early evening snack, and I climb to my little apartment over the garage clutching the Sarah Orne Jewett book that Carol has given me for my library. I will cherish it.

Chapter 38

I pop out of bed, fully rested, and gaze out onto the lake. It is another beautiful morning. I'm ready to get home. This has been a wonderful break, but Sisu and Skip are back at home, and I am looking forward to holing up again with my art. I have new inspiration pushing me to create again. I hope Carol can take some time today to drive me back out to the cabin. I strip the bed and gather my used towels to make it easier for Carol to launder them. I tidy up the room and get my few new clothes and pajamas packed and ready to go. I'll go down to breakfast and she and I can talk about it.

As I carry the laundry bag though the breezeway, I call out "Good mor….." A glance to the right, however, and I see a strange, black car in the driveway. She's probably counseling someone, so I will be quiet and come back when the car leaves. I'm curious, though, so I open the door a crack and hear voices. Carol's high voice and a man's deep voice. I freeze and my heartbeat quickens. They are not discussing personal matters. They are discussing ME! I hear the man say my name.

Closing the door quietly, I stand frozen in place. *Protect yourself, Jenna!* A tidal wave of emotions floods over me: anger, fear, betrayal, danger. This has all been a set up.

I thought she loved me. I loved her. What kind of a monster would trap me here and then call the cops on me? With eyes blurry from hot tears, I retreat up the stairs to grab my coat and hat. I have to get out of here—now. My mind spins. Where will I go? I can't go back to the cabin, even if I hitch a ride. She will know I am there. Maybe Skip will hide me until I figure out a plan, but that won't work for long because she knows where he lives, too. Hands trembling, I fumble to pull on my boots and hat. I'm going to have to go on the run again. I have no choice. Why can't people just leave me alone!

I descend the stairs two at a time and my eyes are playing tricks on me. Standing at the bottom with a serious look on his face is Skip! I run into his arms. "You've to get me out of here! Carol has trapped me and I hate her. She's called someone to take me back, but I won't go! I won't go! Let me out the door! Help me, Skip."

He holds me closely, too closely, in his strong arms—a bear hug. His eyes are sad. I violently push back and try to escape his embrace. "Not you, too? I trusted you. You're family, Skip. How could you do this to me? I hate you, too. Let go of me!" I try to fight him off, hitting his arms and shoulders, slapping his face. I scream at the top of my lungs. My hair whips into my eyes. I am too enraged to cry, but he cries out, and I hear running footsteps.

They have me. I can't overpower Skip now, but I will find my chance later. *Think, think, Jenna.*

"Jenna, stop!" Carol cries out in agony. "It's going to be okay!"

"How can you say that, you double crossing witch? All that talk about loving each other, pinkie swears, the soft bed, the good food, the stupid church service that means NOTHING! It means NOTHING!" My heart is pounding, every nerve on fire, my face burning with rage.

Skip turns me in his embrace, my back to his chest now, and we slide to the tile floor. In exhaustion, I lay my head back and I feel his chin whiskers atop my head. A strange man in a black suit is hanging back in the hall with a shocked expression on his face. He must be social services. When he gets me in his car to take me away, I will jump out and run, or, better yet, overpower him and drive off in his frickin', fancy, black car. *Okay, that's the plan. Look at everything I've planned and done in the last two years. I can do this.*

I feel Skip's strong heart pounding. This is a nightmare. I glance at his pale, shocked face over my shoulder. I whisper, "I won't fight anymore. Let me go, really."

Skip loosens his arms and I stand up. Carol helps Skip awkwardly rise from the floor. He has a red mark on his face where I slapped him. I may have hurt him, but, who cares? He betrayed me.

Carol is first to find her voice. "We all need to calm down and get our wits about us. Mr. Tucker is not here to take you away. He has something important to tell you, Jenna, and you must try to listen. Come and sit. Breathe, everyone."

I need water. I need to sit. I don't know if I can listen because my brain is still so crowded with frantic thoughts, but over all the noise in my head, I hear Uncle Bill. *Listen to what they have to say, Jenna. You've got sisu. Sisu, sisu. Remember.* I sip from a glass of water and then sit on a dining room chair, arms on knees, head down. I can't look at these people.

"Jenna, Mr. Tucker needs to ask you some questions."

"Is your name Jenna Louise Burke?"

"Yeah."

"Where were you born?"

"Someplace in northern Indiana on July 4, 2002."

"What is your mother's full name?"

"Alissa Lehto Burke."

"Is she living?"

"No. She died a while ago in Chicago."

"Have you been living on your own since then?"

"Yes, with some help from these two people here who I thought were my friends." I raise my head and glare at him. "What's this all about, anyway? I'm sick of answering your stupid questions."

"Well, Jenna, I'm John Tucker. I was your Uncle Bill's lawyer and friend for many years. I have been trying to find you since his death. I think we should let you gather your composure before I go on. I need to know you are mature enough to listen carefully and accept fully what I am about to say. First, though, you need to make peace with these two friends here. If it weren't for them, I would never have found you. They both love you very much. It has been obvious from their work on your behalf during the past six months, since you turned sixteen."

I still can't do it. My heart is aching, and the alarm bells are still clanging in my head. "C'mon, tell me what you need to say. I want to get out of here as soon as I can."

"Okay, I get it, Jenna. I know you have been through a lot and have had to fend for yourself. You have just begun to get your life together, and I'm afraid springing this meeting on you was a very bad idea on my part. If you need to blame someone, please blame me. I rushed this meeting before Carol and Skip thought you were ready. Now I know they were right, but we are together now and are braving the storm. You are surrounded by family in this room. Now, let's hear from your Uncle Bill, who loved you, too."

He pulled some papers from his briefcase and began to read in a somber voice. *Being in sound mind and body, this is my last will and testament. I, William Lehto leave my total estate to my sister, Alissa Lehto Burke. If, at the settlement of my estate, Alissa Lehto Burke is not living, I bequeath the totality of my estate to her daughter, my niece, Jenna Louise Burke, born July 4, 2002. John Tucker is named as my executor.*

Anger is turning to sadness. My whole body aches at Uncle Bill's words. "What does this all mean?"

Mr. Tucker puts down the will and leans toward me, elbows on knees. I focus on his argyle socks. His voice is gentle and quiet. "This means you have inherited Loon Haven. The property consists of 80 acres, a cabin and a pond. You also own the proceeds from a life insurance policy and Bill's personal effects that have been in storage in Marquette since his death. I've been using the interest generated by the policy to pay the property taxes on the acreage the last four years, and have put the remainder in a savings account for your mother. Skip came to me last July and reported the death of your mom, which I verified from official records. At the same time, I located your birth certificate. Turning sixteen allows you to inherit the estate. Jenna, your Uncle Bill and I were classmates in high school, and I knew your mother well, too. I have been holding on to hope I would find you and your mom to give you this news. I remember how much your grandpa, Bill, and Alissa loved the camp. We had some great poker games there."

He smiled—but I'm not in the mood. Being reminded the people I love are all dead is not what I want to hear right now. "So, I'm still a kid. Can anyone take the camp away from me?" I finally fully meet his gaze. His eyes are light blue and kind. I sense a growing excitement behind them. He sits forward and tries to hold my hands, but I'm not having it. I don't know this man.

He withdraws his hands and sits back. "Nope. Here's all we have to do. In Michigan, you can be emancipated from your parents when you turn sixteen. Someone has to sign an affidavit saying it is their opinion you can live independently. Carol, as a pastor, can sign this for you. The three of us believe that from the income from the insurance policy, along with the sales of your improving art work, and the occasional family support of Carol and Skip, you can continue to live on your property, if you want to. As an emancipated teen, you have the right to own, buy and sell property, change your name, manage your money the way you see fit—really everything an adult can do—except buy alcohol, vote, and drive a car, which I understand, you actually do better than the pastor, here." His efforts to make us laugh fall flat, his lonely chuckle echoes around the big room.

"What about having to go to school?"

"That's totally up to you and only you."

We all sit in silence for a while. I'm numb, but, suddenly, Carol seems to wake up from a stupor, a smile lights up her face, and her ridiculous ADD kicks in loud and fast. "I'll help her study for her GED!"

The three of them turn toward one another and ideas fill the air like bullets—fast and furious. "She can enroll at the college in Marquette for art classes," Skip exclaims.

"I'll help manage her money," added Mr. Tucker. "As soon as we get her cabin repaired, we can bring back the furniture and things Skip and I stored when Bill died. His old, blue Dodge truck is still under a tarp in my backyard!"

Skip is really getting pumped up. "We can build her a sauna, plumb a little bit, buy her a moped to get to town until she can legally drive. Propane would be good out there. Maybe some solar and a battery setup." Carol and Mr. Tucker are nodding, grinning, and seem to have forgotten I'm even in the room. I can feel my anxiety beginning to rise once again. The tightness in my chest builds, and finally I explode onto my feet.

"Whoa, whoa, whoa—stop—cut it out!" I put my hands over my ears and have to shout to break into the excited chatter. "I've got to think about all this stuff, people! Gimme a break! This is my life—MY LIFE!" I quickly cross the living room to stare out the big window, not seeing the lake beyond, but trying desperately to get away from these three people and the thoughts piling up and jamming my head and heart.

The room falls silent.

I wheel around and walk quickly past the stares. Carol has her arms out to give me an embrace, but I sweep past her and call over my shoulder, "Carol, drive me home—now!"

Our trip over the snow-covered roads passes in silence, just static and music on the radio turned down low. She drops me off at the road with my bags of new clothes and art supplies. I lean in her window and give her a kiss on the cheek. It's all I can think to do. I'm totally drained, and I can tell she is, too.

She speaks softly to me. "I don't think Skip and I need apologize for loving you too much, and we do love you. I can see why you feel betrayed. I should have asked your permission to invite Mr. Tucker to the house. I broke my promise to you. My actions were selfish. I got carried away with what I want for you and forgot it is what you want for yourself that matters. We all make mistakes. I need your forgiveness. There would have been a better time and place to talk to you about all of this in a gentler way, but I don't think any of us—even you—could have anticipated that such fears, sorrow, and anger were lurking so close to the surface, ready to explode." Her eyes were brimming with tears.

"A lot of life just came crashing down on me today, Carol. When I panicked, I did and said things I'm not proud of. I don't even remember most of it. I need time to think. Is that okay?"

"Ah, my dear. Take all the time you need. You are home now…and safe. Loon Haven will help you continue to heal."

Her frosty window rolls up. She gives me a sad smile and a wave, and is off, slowly this time. I watch her go, tires crunching in the snow and the exhaust from the tailpipe billowing in white clouds behind her. I stoop to grab the handles of my bags and begin the walk up the lane.

Pine needles glisten on each side of me, and, as I turn into the yard, I hear a friendly whistle—Sisu! She has been waiting for me and welcomes me home. "I'll get you a treat as soon as I can, little friend. You have no idea how I have missed you. I've missed you too, old cabin." The cabin is settled deep in snowdrifts, icicles dangle from the edge of the roof. Lonely, dark windows greet me like lifeless eyes. I lurch up the steps under my burden of bags. The door swings open and the ice-cold stove contrasts with the warm paintings and drawings hanging on every wall. Brrr. The cabin and I are suddenly both chilled to the bone.

I put my hands to familiar work and soon there is a crackling fire burning in the stove radiating heat to every corner of the room and beginning to drive out the chill. I give Sisu her snack of birdseed, and she performs an extra happy dance on the snowy woodpile and up and down my forearm. I smile for the first time since losing my cool back in Birch Bay. This is where I belong.

It's sort of weird, though. As I gaze back at the cabin, smoke curling from the chimney, and at the frozen pond bisected by stitches of fox tracks, surely I should be doing a happy dance, too. I own this land and this cabin, and this pond, and this crooked outhouse. It all belongs to me on a piece of paper. I saw the paper with my own eyes. I saw Uncle Bill's signature. Lots of teenagers would love to be emancipated, have a source of money, a roof over their heads, their independence, making their own decisions, not having to show up for school.

I feel empty and lonely, instead. Setting down my bags, I sadly climb the ladder down to the root cellar, close and lock the trap door, and go to bed in total darkness—without reading—without thinking—without dreaming.

Chapter 39

I'm just going through the motions. I haven't touched a paintbrush since I got back. I haven't carved a notch, but it has had to have been two weeks since I have spoken to anyone other than Sisu. I spend my days dressed in layers by the stove, fur hat on my head, feeding the fire one log after another to keep the cabin somewhat warm, battling the snowy and windy days and nights. The snow is drifted halfway up my windows, blocking what little daylight there is. I sit and watch my beans and rice simmer in the dark room, gazing at the steam rising from the pot and only going outside to use the outhouse and bring in more wood. I leaf through the pages of the *Mother Earth News*, but the words just seem to drift past my eyes. I sleep long hours in the total darkness of the root cellar; the days are short and sunless. I have absolutely no energy or joy.

It's another dreary afternoon. When I head outside to bring in some wood, I catch a glimpse of a red and black lumberjack coat. Skip is standing on the other side of the pond. He's looking at me but doesn't move. After several minutes, he slowly raises a mittened hand. I return the gesture. How can I talk to this man—a man I hit and slapped and insulted and then walked out on?

We stood in silence for a long time, then he called, "Jenna, may I come on?"

"Yes," I turn toward the cabin. I stomp off my boots, dump the wood on the floor, and begin to fill the coffeepot. I hear him clumping up the porch steps and shedding his coat and hat.

"Want some coffee?"

"Sure. If you're making it for yourself."

"Sure has been cold lately." The weather is always a safe topic.

"Yep. Sure has been. Mind if I smoke?"

"Nah. Go ahead." The familiar fragrance of his cherry tobacco soon fills the air.

We sit, drink, and look at the fire in silence.

Finally, he speaks. "It's PTSD, you know."

"What are you talking about?"

"Post-Traumatic Stress Disorder. It's been a problem for me since Iraq, and I saw it in you the other day. Lots of my buddies suffered from it. When you and I were sittin' there on the floor, strugglin' with each other, both of us out of our right minds, a sense of déjà vu hit me. I've been there before, Jenna. I've had the same sort of fear, sense of betrayal, pain, and exhaustion take over my life for moments, days, and weeks."

"What are you saying? I'm crazy?"

"That's what I used to ask the docs, too. I thought they were accusin' me of being weak."

"Well, weren't they?"

"They finally got it through my thick skull that PTSD can be a common reaction to chronic stress—day after day pressure in life-threatenin' conditions, like war, or, in your case, life on the streets with a sick and dyin' mom. The thing is, you would think once a person gets out of the bad situation, it would all go away—but it doesn't. I have had episodes of insomnia, nightmares, and acting out in anger. Sometimes I don't remember much about what I have said and done. Freak outs, I call 'em. I have fewer of them, as the years go by, but they are always scary and leave me confused and emptied out. I have to depend on the people around me to understand and to forgive me for what I say and do sometimes. Around here, they just chalk it up as a character flaw, and we all have 'em in the UP."

I took a deep breath and nodded. He was making some sense.

"Glad to be home?"

"I would be gladder if my feet weren't freezing and my heart wasn't so empty. I don't feel like doing anything, Skip. I can't read. I don't have any appetite. I'm just so sad. Is the sun EVER going to come out again?"

"A hard winter like this one can do that to you up here, but you are goin' to be okay. You've got sisu, eh?"

"Sure don't feel much like it. I don't remember much about my freak out, as you call it, but I know I tried to hurt you."

"Ahh, don't fret about that. I've had bigger and meaner people poundin' on me. You didn't even make a dent in this old hide."

"I'm glad," I sighed. I don't want to lose Skip or Carol.

"Do you think Carol understands?"

"Yeah. I talked to her about my PTSD once when she put her little scrawny self between me and another fellow when we were comin' to blows over somethin' stupid. She dragged me into her church office and we hashed it out. I reminded her of that after she got back from bringin' you home. She was still pretty shook up and was blamin' herself for ambushin' you. She is afraid you are never goin' to forgive her… or that you might pack up and disappear. I told her we should just give you some time and that I would keep an eye on you from afar to make sure you were doin' okay. She said she would pray hard for us all. You know, she believes that works, and I'm all for it, if it does."

I let out a great sigh. "Thanks, Skip—for talking."

"I'll always be here for you, Jenna. Don't ever forget that. It would take a lot more than a little wrestlin' match to keep me from lovin' you." His voice faltered, and he looked away, pretending to study one of my paintings while I wiped my eyes with the back of my hand.

"Okay. Enough sappy talk. Do you have enough food in the house to get you through the next couple of weeks? We'll be havin' a thaw about then, and maybe some sunshine to go with it. I'm gonna hole up at the house and tie some flies until then, try to keep my chickens from layin' frozen eggs. You be okay?" He grinned.

"Yeah, I've got plenty of food in the root cellar. Why don't you come back the first sunny day and bring those flies. I would like to try fly-fishing this spring. Would you teach me?"

"You betcha! Listen to your good heart. Get back to your paintin', so's you got somethin' new to show me next time, eh?" He pulled on his thick coat, his fur hat and choppers and disappeared into the steadily falling snow.

Chapter 40

I can feel myself somewhere in the hazy zone between waking and sleeping. There is nothing but silence around me, but in the twilight of my mind, Uncle Bill appears vividly before my eyes in his Hawaiian shirt and shorts, fishing pole in hand—a big smile aimed at Mom in her cutoffs and sweatshirt, bare feet! She brings in his stringer of fish to clean for dinner, swings it around and comes straight at me! I see it all—I hear it all—their faces, their clothes, their laughter. Now, I become a soaring bird, watching this scene from above. The cabin is neat and tidy. A forest green canoe is dragged up on the beach, a pair of loons are cruising along the far shore of the pond. The female has her babies riding on her back. Now the scene changes again in a flash. I'm a kid playing with dominos on the porch floor. Uncle Bill puts his fishing pole down and sits in the rocker. He smiles down at me. Mom soon joins him, carrying a can of beer for each of them. I can smell his tobacco and his fishy hands. Mom's voice is clear and strong. They are watching me play, laughing and talking about how we are so lucky to be together—in one special place. They toast with their beers, smiling, and tapping them. *A toast to Loon Haven. May she go on forever.*

I open my eyes wide in the pitch dark and lie completely still and totally rested. The happy scene dissolves, but I am still floating, warm and comfortable. I savor the memory of those faces and voices. I want to grasp their hands and keep them here with me—those people I love and who love me still. Somewhere, somehow.

They are sending me a message of hope, and the same flash of inspiration that guides my paintbrush floods my heart and mind. I get it. This place doesn't belong to me—it belongs to us—past, present, and future! Loon Haven is the sum total of everyone who has ever danced on her cabin floors or pulled a perch from her water. Mr. Tucker, who played poker at the kitchen table. Skip, who loved my mother with a passion that has had no end and loves me in turn. Mom, who relished her time here in the summers. Carol, who has held my art work as if she were holding a precious child. My grandfather, who worked the timber, built this cabin with his son, and helped to keep the place going until the day he died.

In the mists of time, there was a grandmother whose name is my own, and great-grandparents who ventured from Finland to the deep forests of northern Michigan. I have but discovered the key that will open the door to my life here. That locked door has been bothering my heart and mind since hearing of my inheritance. Deep down, I questioned if I was worthy or capable to accept the challenge, but I am the caretaker of a precious gift from my family. I can do hard things. I will not let them down. I've got sisu!

I spring out of that cellar, carrying coffee and supplies to make a big breakfast. I stoke up the stove, and wolf down a big bowl of hot oatmeal with dried thimbleberries and brown sugar and then make myself another. I'm famished, and this is so, so delicious. Life is delicious! Bill's spirit is back beside me. I smile because he knows I have a plan. I have passed an invisible boundary, and I'm large and in charge again. I stand on my chair to carve the last notch on the doorframe. These precious notches represent my day-by-day past, but my future here doesn't need to be counted. It is unlimited and certain. I realize I am grinning from ear to ear.

Enough grinning and loafing around, Jenna. Uncle Bill's voice is urging me on. I hop down from my chair, drag it in front of the warm stove, pull my sketchbook and a pencil on my lap. Time to dream! Time to plan!

Plans for Loon Haven

First, a heartfelt apology to Carol. Ask her to help me contact Mr. Tucker. I want to start the paperwork to change my name to Jenna Alissa Lehto.

Design a cabin restoration exactly the way I want it with the big tree removed, the kitchen and bedroom loft restored, a new roof and insulation.

A small addition to the west side of the house will serve as a studio for me. Add on a room for a composting toilet now, plumbing later. I will turn the outhouse into a tool shed. Sorry, Grandpa. After all, this is going to be my home, and a girl needs a few creature comforts.

If funds allow, buy a canoe (green), materials for a sauna, a bucket from Kaarlo to put inside.

Water well and a hand pump in the kitchen.

Maybe a solar battery setup to provide power down the line in the future. I saw that in *Mother Earth News.*

This is going to be awesome! Each idea excites me more. I am warm all over for the first time in weeks. My blood is circulating again. My brain has finally thawed out and is firing away, at last. I can't wait to finish the painting over there on the easel.

Whoa, there! I had better find out my financial situation before I get too carried away with building my castle in the air. My trusty copy of *Walden* is within reach. Haven't looked at what Henry has to say in a long time, but Uncle Bill has stuck a feather in a page at the very end of the book. As I turn to the last page, the rare winter sun sends a shaft of dusty yellow light onto the floorboards by the stove, and I read…

The light which puts out our eyes is darkness to us. Only that day dawns to which we are awake. There is more day to dawn. The sun is but a morning star.

Resources: Learn More About It

Walden by Henry David Thoreau
Drawing the Head and Hands by Andrew Loomis
Taking the Leap by Pema Chodron
Sisu: The Finnish Art of Courage by Joanna Nylund
Yooper Talk by Kathryn A. Remlinger
Images of America: Finns of Michigan's Upper Peninsula, forward by Kay Seppala
A White Heron by Sarah Orne Jewett

Search on-line: Finnish axes, Stormy Kromer hats, porcupine quillwork, Anishinaabe, Finnish cabin building, building an outdoor sauna, birch tree swinging, Finnish fabric design, crow intelligence, gray jay, Post-Traumatic Stress Disorder

The author welcomes your questions and comments at sylduncan@hotmail.com. She is also available to join your book group discussions regarding *My Escape to Loon Haven* via Zoom or to make local appearances in Michigan at libraries or bookstores. This book can be obtained through Amazon.com in both paperback and ebook format.

Acknowledgements

Special thanks to Sue Walker, who listened and added insight to the story that was forming in my brain five years ago, and who encouraged me to create Jenna out of thin air. A thank you to my early readers for their encouragement and suggestions. To my husband, Tom, who has spent over fifty years teaching me the value of self-reliance and a love for the natural world. To the wonderful people Tom and I have met and the places we've traveled in the unique and amazing Upper Peninsula of Michigan, notably our dear friend The Reverend Carolyn Raffensperger and the fine people of Big Bay.

This book is dedicated to my son Andrew, daughter-in-law Marie, and my grandchildren, Tucker and Lila, all of whom have sisu.

Cover art image provided by Shutterstock

Made in USA - Crawfordsville, IN
62091_9798354653560
11.16.2022 1346